ANGEL STRIKES

SOUL FORGE BOOK FOUR

LESLIE CLAIRE WALKER

sfp

My name is Night Sanchez. Every choice I make is a fight against fate.

As the gears turn for the coming apocalypse, my destiny is tied to the Angel of Death's. I don't know whether a way out exists—only that I haven't found one yet. But my purpose is clear.

To keep my people safe. To make sure none of those brave beloveds try to follow me over the edge of the apocalyptic cliff.

Even if it means conquering an archangel.

The Archangel Gabriel seeks warriors for the coming cosmic battle, and he sets his sights on unsuspecting normals. They may not belong to me, but I'll rally behind them.

I'll risk my soul for theirs, and Red will put his heart on the line, too. But what if heart and soul are not enough? Can we defeat not only Gabriel, but destiny itself?

Watch us.

ALSO BY LESLIE CLAIRE WALKER

THE AWAKENED MAGIC SAGA

THE SOUL FORGE

(The Complete Series)

Angel Hunts

Angel Rises

Angel Falls

Angel Strikes

Angel Roars

Angel Burns

THE FAERY CHRONICLES

(The Complete Series)

Faery Novice

Faery Prophet

Faery Sovereign

SHORT STORY COLLECTIONS

Ink & Blood

Ink & Stars

Ink & Sword

For Chester

CHAPTER 1

T HE WIND GUSTED, pushing an empty beer bottle along the concrete. A stink of motor oil and the ghost of patchouli incense hung in the air. The engine of the yellow Volkswagen behind us ticked impatience as it cooled. Its headlights flooded the alley in which we stood, lighting up the red brick walls of the buildings on either side.

One entrance. One exit. Limited sightlines from my vantage at the mouth of the alley. Easy to defend, and unsettling. The air itself seemed to tremble. Powerful people with powerful magic filled the alley, but my vision and all of my other senses narrowed to one.

Faith.

She stood in front of the old school bus that crouched at the back of the alley, its metal and glass form wavering in and out of sight. The twinkle lights that hung in the open windows gave off enough illumination that I could see her face clearly in the dark.

Her brown eyes shone with joy and relief—I saw my daughter in them, a seventeen-year-old girl, glad to see me. She looked like my kid, too, in black jeans and boots, bright gold sweater over a black tank. Long black hair hung in waves over her shoulders. Her light brown skin glowed with health. My hourglass pendant dangled at her throat.

The rest of the world fell away. Smells and tastes and dimension-spanning school buses faded from my sight. My magic met Faith's halfway across the distance between us, and the feel of her power, mingled with that of the god she carried, warmed the lingering chill of my grief.

Then my senses expanded again, taking in everything and every-one. I heard a sharp intake of breath to my right—Faith's girlfriend, Corey, took off toward Faith at a run, her fire-engine-red bob a streak in the night. Her footfalls echoed through the alley and then ceased as she vaulted into Faith's arms, squeezing her tight and planting a kiss on Faith's mouth.

"Thank all the powers," my lover, Red, whispered. He leaned into my left side, reaching for my hand and twining his fingers with mine. Breathing in the grass and earth of his magic steadied me.

I studied as much of Faith as I could see. Her halo—the life force that flowed through her and manifested as an aura of light around her body—glowed with the silver that announced the flavor of her unique magic, the ability to speak with gods. Threads of gold shot through the silver, woven so tightly that they had become part of her, served as a reminder that she was no longer just a girl with magic. She carried a god known as the Awakened inside of her. The god of magic.

The god had come fully awake in her a handful of days ago. She'd vanished like so much smoke in that moment, leaving me grief-stricken and worried beyond imagining about what had happened to her. What could happen to her.

She looked all right.

I spoke my own thanks silently to all the powers who'd brought her back to us unharmed. Two of them stood in the alley with us.

Beside the bus's door stood a man sculpted from raw power. He wore a black knit cap on his bald head, a black tank, black leather pants, and motorcycle boots. His black leather trench coat dusted the ground. His skin was so pale, it was almost translucent. His gray eyes that had seen everything—literally, everything—from the dawn of time. He had no halo at all. I'd never seen a being without one, but then, he wasn't just anyone.

He had to be Malek, the serpent from the Garden of Eden. He'd been cursed into human form and had walked the world since the dawn of time. Whoever had cursed him had stolen his ability to speak. No more tempting humans with pretty words.

I'd learned about him during my training with the Order of the Blood Moon. His apprentice, Beth, had told me a bit more.

She had moved to stand at the tail end of the bus, her brown hair a bird's nest of braids. Every inch of her red T-shirt was covered with pictures of comic-style Christmas elves yelling four-letter words. Black threads snaked through her bright orange halo.

They'd brought us here under false pretenses, telling me I could see the kids that Red and I had saved from being magically drained by my former masters at the Order of the Blood Moon. I'd needed to see them. To make sure they were okay. To tell them that their magic was a gift that belonged to them, not to those who would exploit it. And when we'd arrived, they'd made with the bait-and-switch.

I looked at Beth. "Why didn't you tell me Faith was here?" I asked. "Why keep it from me?"

Malek raised his hands to sign, to answer me. *The bus serves as a sanctuary for the magical children. It wavers in your sight because it's rooted in Faery, but visiting here. The magic that created this is new and precarious.*

"That's not a reason," I said.

Faith rested her chin on Corey's shoulder. The corners of her mouth trembled. "I'm the reason."

I met her gaze. "You didn't want them to call me."

She shook her head.

The relief I'd felt a moment ago fled.

She pulled away from Corey and took a step toward me. "It's not because I didn't want to see you. It's because we've got trouble, and I wanted to try to figure it out on my own first. I can't carry a god on my shoulders and then run to my mom every time something comes up."

I blinked at her. I could pick all of that apart, but I wouldn't. For one, she'd called me Mom—a rare thing. And two, Faith was almost grown. The only way to *be* grown was to make mistakes and learn from them. My worry about whether she'd come out okay, much less unscathed, was my own, not hers. No matter how hard it felt, and no matter the intensity of the stakes.

"I get it," I said.

She took a deep breath and blew it out slowly.

"What's the trouble?" I asked.

"It's Sunday's friend," she said. "Charlie Nobody?"

Sunday hadn't come with us, opting to stay in Portland with the rest of the team to help defend them against any incoming attacks. All the powers knew we had enough enemies who might take my absence as opportunity. If they were stupid enough to underestimate Sunday Sloan. I'd been the number-two magical assassin in the Order of the Blood Moon's ranks. Sunday had been number one. She used her magic to blind her targets and her considerable fighting skills to kill. She was my best friend, and my former lover.

Before the Order had taken her in, she'd met a time-traveling kid by the name of Charlie Nobody. He'd resurfaced a few days ago and had been momentarily trapped by Order operatives. I'd wondered what had happened to him.

"What about him?" I asked.

"He's here," Faith said. "On the bus. And he's sick."

Inside my rib cage, in the space around my heart, the magical being I hosted—the Angel of Death—caught my attention with a flutter of wings. Their physical counterpart—the black-feathered wings sprouting from my shoulder blades—itched. "Magical sickness?"

"Yeah," she said. "He's the one who insisted I call you. He said we need the Angel. Said we wouldn't be able to stop what's coming without him."

The Angel's voice sounded in my mind, echoing with the vastness of eternity. *If this sickness is what I think it is, it was caused by another Horseman.*

Another one? I had enough to handle with the Angel.

There are four, he said.

I was no Biblical scholar and, in any case, things didn't work as written in that book. It was more like a puzzle to unravel than a literal instruction manual or a true prophecy, all of it filtered through the human prejudices and character flaws of the men who wrote it. The Horsemen were part of the puzzle, as was the coming Apocalypse.

The Four Horsemen of the Apocalypse: *La Muerte,* whom I carried. The one who would eventually reap all the souls in all the worlds, and the souls of the worlds themselves.

Famine, who wore a little girl's body as her vessel. Famine had a way of knowing what people craved in the deepest, most hidden parts of their souls, and she gave it to them. She trapped them. Fed off their hunger. Kept them until there was nothing left.

The other two, I had yet to meet. War. And Pestilence.

Had to be that last one.

Is the sickness catching? I asked.

It shouldn't be.

I waited for more. The Angel said nothing. Which either meant he didn't know, or he couldn't or wouldn't tell me right now.

That's shitty, I said.

He had no reply.

Even if the illness wasn't catching as I understood it, a sense of urgency took root in the bowl of my belly.

I aimed my out-loud voice at Faith. "Charlie Nobody's on the bus?"

She nodded.

I glanced at Red from the corner of my eye, taking in his grass-green and earth-brown halo, the salt-and-pepper of his shaggy hair and mustache, and the sharp concern behind his green eyes. He'd unzipped his gray hoodie. I could see the flames of his sacred heart tattoo above the collar of his white T-shirt.

There was more there than a normal love connection—or the usual connection between people with magic. Red and I shared a heart connection that had been forged in love and cemented in grief. Time had done nothing to fade it. On top of that, the magic we'd created together a couple of days ago, binding the magic of each person in our team into one clear, powerful, multifaceted channel of power, and the mind connection that had been part of that spell, hadn't entirely faded either.

I had no way to know how much he'd caught of my conversation with the Angel or my own thoughts about it. He'd gleaned enough, and he knew how I felt.

Red squeezed my hand and let go, squaring his shoulders, faint Texas accent painting his words. "Let's see the kid."

Faith turned on her heel and led Corey through the open door and up the steps. Red and I followed, pausing for a disorienting moment as we came within twenty feet of the bus. The air rippled like water, as if we were stones skipped along its surface. The bus and concrete—and the edges of Malek's and Beth's skin, too—glowed with blue fire. Then the moment passed. The fire winked out, and the air steadied, as if it had tasted us and allowed us to stay.

I took the bus steps two at a time, Red on my heels, expecting to see ripped and scratched vinyl seats and a narrow aisle in between, the strings of lights twinkling in the windows. Instead, I walked into a long corridor with stone walls and a polished oak floor so old, I took a second to wonder why it hadn't petrified. Tall oak doors had been built into the walls at ten-foot intervals, all of them closed. The double doors at the end of the hall were open, though. An invitation.

Too many points of attack between where we stood and that open door. And no sign of Faith or Corey.

Behind me, Red muttered, "The fuck?"

"Faery," I said. "Has to be."

He whistled. "Malek said the bus was half in our world, and half in Faery."

"No lie."

Red stuck out a hand behind him, waving it toward the invisible door we'd just stepped through. He stretched to cover the width of the hall with his reach.

"It's gone," he said. "The door's gone."

I let my magic rise, feeling the waves of my own power as they crested. I could slip into any mind, inserting myself into memories and dreams. I could take control of my targets. Drop them into their worst nightmares and leave them there to languish and die. The Order of the Blood Moon had trained me to use my magic to kill. I'd excelled at it.

That had been another life, one I'd chosen to leave no matter what it cost me. But thanks to the unfolding end of the world and the part I played in it—much of which remained a mystery—I'd come to terms with who I'd been, with the fate that had overtaken me, and with what I wanted to become.

I didn't expect an attack. But better safe than sorry.

The Angel murmured his approval.

"Let's go," I said.

Red walked at my side, the thud of our footfalls echoing against wood and stone. The hallway remained empty. No surprises, other than that the open doors at the end of the hall appeared to grow in height the closer we got, topping out at around thirty feet, solid oak, floor-to-ceiling. The oak was carved with images of animals. Bucks. Fish. Owls. Every kind of tree I'd ever seen, and a bunch I hadn't.

At the threshold, the same strange ripple we'd experienced at the bus's magical perimeter happened again. One second, the air changed and time slowed. The next, we stepped into a room a hundred feet wide and three hundred feet long. Torches in full flame lined the walls, their light pushing all the shadows in the space into the corners. At the far end, a handful of steps led to a platform with deep green moss for carpet and simple oak chairs for thrones. Empty ones, at that.

The person who ought to have sat in one of them had hunkered down in front of it. I'd never met him, but his halo told the story—it was the color of forest loam after a rain, and practically screamed royalty. The Faery King, white-feathered wings folded neatly behind his back, focused all of his attention on my kid, who knelt along with Corey in front of the prone form of a child laid flat before them.

The Faery King glanced up as Red and I approached the platform and met my gaze with brown eyes that held the gathered power of an entire world. The front of his short brown hair dusted his eyelashes.

He wore a crisp white long-sleeve shirt and a brown leather vest with slits to accommodate the aforementioned wings. Brown leather pants. Brown leather boots on his feet. He looked uncomfortable in the clothes, as if he would've preferred something simpler.

He was barely older than Faith. Maybe a year. Jesus Christ.

His voice was Joe Normal, not what I imagined Faery King might be. "Night, thanks for coming."

He waved for us to come closer and be quick about it, moving to make room for us as we climbed the stairs. Stepping onto the moss-covered platform felt like stepping onto the forest floor, only one I'd never experienced before. The crush of green under my feet, the freshness of the air I drew into my lungs, the small talk of insects—they spoke of something so old and protected, it'd never been seen by humans.

I knelt in the space beside the Faery King, and Red sank to one knee on my left, next to Faith.

The king stuck out his hand. "Kevin."

I shook it. "Weird name for a fae. Weird gesture for a fae."

"I wasn't always." He pointed at the boy who lay in front of us. "This is Charlie."

Charlie looked fourteen or fifteen, a bit older than when Sunday first met him. His unruly hair looked as if it were made of gold. Pale skin flushed red, and his hazel eyes shone with fever. He wore a used-to-be-white button-down with the sleeves rolled up to his elbows and a pair of dark gray trousers that had been mended more times than I could count, with suspenders to hold them up. A dark gray porkpie hat rested on his belly, his fingers dancing along the brim. His feet were bare and dirty. His halo had a greenish cast to it that had nothing to do with his magic and everything to do with what ailed him.

Red laid a palm on Charlie's forehead. "That's some fever."

"Thanks," Charlie croaked.

Red cracked a smile that Charlie tried to answer, not too successfully.

"It's okay to look at me like you want to," Charlie said.

Using magic, which would allow Red to see deep into a person's heart and soul, past all masks, pretenses, and defenses, down to who they truly were. Red saw the beauty in people who couldn't see it in themselves.

"The illness," he said, "doesn't just affect your body. It's tied to your soul."

Charlie nodded. "I'm up shit creek."

"Pestilence," I said. "*La Muerte* says it was the Horseman that did this."

Kevin nodded.

"I have to ask why Charlie is still sick," I said. "In my training with the Order, I was told a myth about the being in the center of the planet that dreams all the worlds into form. How the fae channel those dreams and shape them before they become embodied in a person or place or thing. You should be able to catch hold of the dream of this sickness and reshape it into health, right?"

"Not too many humans know that lore," Kevin said. "But I can't heal him. Maybe because what's ailing him—the dream—isn't coming from the Dreamer in the Land." He cocked his head at Faith.

She took over the telling. "And I can't cure Charlie either. He's got magic, and the sickness is magical. The Awakened is the god of magic. So, we should be able to separate the sickness from his magic, or alter the magic so that it rejects the sickness. But we can't."

Charlie cleared his throat. "Night?"

I met his gaze.

"The Horseman's not born into this world yet," Charlie said. "It was hunting a human vessel in my town, in my when. It didn't just do this to me. It did it to all of us. All of the magical kids I've been collecting."

Elder beings like the Horsemen were powerful in their own right before they took human vessels. But they couldn't walk in our world without one. They couldn't act in our world without one. If the Horseman had been hunting—

"Pestilence found its vessel there?" I asked.

"No," Charlie said. "None of us was the right one for him. I jumped into the timestream and aimed for right here and right now, looking for a safe space to bring my people. He followed me through and then took off. I tracked him for as long as I could, and saw where he was headed, but the sickness took over and I had to leave off. That's when I came here. I aimed for a place where I could get help."

"You did good," I said. "Where was Pestilence headed?"

"Portland," he said.

I blinked at him. "My Portland? West or east?"

"West. Sorry to say."

I reached down to brush the damp hair from his brow. "We're gonna figure this out."

Charlie nodded.

I met Red's gaze. I saw my thoughts mirrored behind his eyes.

If Pestilence had woven an illness this strong into Charlie Nobody's soul before bothering to take up residence inside a vessel, then what he could do from inside a human host would be that much worse.

And right now, according to Charlie, Pestilence was heading to my adopted city. I needed to call. To give everyone at home a head's up. Right now.

"Cell service down here?"

Kevin pressed his lips into a thin line.

So, no. "We need to get back to the human world."

He nodded. "You should take Charlie with you. I've been keeping him safe, hiding him here since he showed up. You're the only person who can move him and keep him safe once he leaves Faery."

My brow furrowed. "Me?"

"Because of the Angel," Kevin said.

I nodded. It always came down to the Angel. "Another Horseman is unlikely to come after me. They'd be going up against someone equally powerful."

Kevin shook his head. "Not equally. The Angel of Death is the most powerful of the Horsemen. He's the oldest, too. I wouldn't let that go to your head, though."

"That's the last place I'd let it go to," I said. "We're still talking about Horsemen of the Apocalypse. The Angel and I aren't exactly a well-oiled machine. We're still figuring things out."

"Yeah." For a second, it seemed he had something more to say, but something preempted that. He turned to glance toward the double doors, rising out of his crouch.

I followed his gaze to a guy about Kevin's age, six feet tall with a bright orange buzz cut, striding down the center of the great room in a pair of dirty white Chucks, battle-scarred blue jeans, and a neon-orange-and-lime-green Hawaiian shirt that must've taken balls of steel just to put on this morning. He had an air of authority and a halo that shone like a rainbow.

A faery seer—a human who could see the fae, along with angels and demons. Faery seers acted as magical law enforcement, tracking non-human magical beings who entered the human world inside their territory and sending any who meant harm back where they'd come from.

The seer's gaze grazed me, appraising, before moving on to mark the rest of us and settling on Kevin. The seer's voice rang out loud. "Dude. You were supposed to wait for me."

Kevin set his hands on his hips, unfurling his wings to half-staff. "Not my problem you couldn't be on time, man. The next Horseman isn't going to wait for you, either."

The seer jogged toward us, not bothering with the steps up to the platform. He jumped instead. "You told me you were bringing help, Kev. You didn't say who."

Kevin rolled his eyes. "Everybody, this is Rude. Rude, this is Corey, Red, and Night. And the Angel of Death."

I'd never met anyone named for bad behavior, and no one had ever introduced the Angel as if he were a person. And I didn't like that Kevin had, although I couldn't put my finger on why. I raised a brow.

Kevin shrugged.

Rude inclined his head toward me. "How do we stop this?"

"Considering we just got here, hell if I know."

Rude flashed a wry grin. "We're supposed to meet at Malek's in ten. There's more going on here than you already know."

"More is fired," Kevin said.

"I know, right?" Rude bent at the waist, holding out a hand for Charlie to take. "Can you stand up? Just for a second?"

Charlie squinted at him. "You're a strange man."

"I'm what there is," Rude said.

Charlie took Rude's hand, and Rude pulled the kid to his feet. Then he scooped the kid into his arms.

That was our signal to go. We rose as a group and followed Rude down the steps and across the length of the long hall, with Faith and Corey at the head and Red in the middle of the group. Kevin and I brought up the end of the line.

"Worried about your friend Sunday?" he asked.

I nodded.

"From what Faith tells me, she can handle herself."

I pressed the heel of my hand to my forehead. "Against everyone she's come up against so far."

"Horsemen?" he asked.

Aside from the Angel of Death, who'd been looking for a way to get to Faith when we'd first encountered him, no. "Not yet."

We passed the threshold of the great room, stepping into the corridor, which was as empty as it'd been before, all the doors on either side of the hallway still closed. And it still felt creepy. Hot on our heels, the beautifully carved oak doors swung shut on well-oiled hinges.

"Got a mind of their own?" I asked.

"If you're asking whether this place is alive and sentient, the answer's yes," he said.

That explained some of the creep factor. "Where's the door that leads out? The door we came in through disappeared behind us."

"A little further along. You have to know what you're looking for."

"Better security," I said.

"Yeah." He slid his hands into the pockets of his leather trousers. "Do they itch much?"

I blinked at him.

"The raised ridges on your back," he said. "They mess up the line of your shirt."

I looked down at the black tank I wore, tucked into my black jeans. I'd thrown a long-sleeve white shirt over the top, leaving it unbuttoned—my only concession to the Houston winter weather, and what I'd thought of as appropriate camouflage for the wings that'd begun to grow out of my shoulder blades. Clearly, I hadn't done as good a job with that as I'd hoped.

"You have some experience with that," I said.

"More than once, although this last time it's permanent."

I didn't want to ask too many questions. We were on the clock and there were more urgent things to worry about that my wings. And "more than once" sounded like a lot of storytelling. I boiled my asks down to one.

"What's it like, becoming something so alien to what you were?"

Kevin mulled the question. "It's weird. I see the world through different eyes, and my priorities are different. I have obligations I'd never imagined. My life isn't my own anymore. It's easy to fall into the idea that it never did belong to me alone, but that's not really true. I was a normal kid. I had a normal, sometimes shitty life. Now, I barely have time to breathe."

"Believe it or not, I understand some of that."

"I bet you do," he said.

Beth had told me that I might not just be hosting the Angel of Death, but that I might become him. I'd never considered that she meant it literally. Anyway, there was always something more important than my feelings or my fears these days. Something or someone that needed my help. I owed it to them to do what I could.

"I don't know what's going on for sure," I said, "only that I didn't ask for these wings. They belong to the Angel. A Horseman. To something that's never been human."

"You bring who you are into whatever you become. Being the Faery King—becoming fae—is not entirely becoming alien. I'm still me. All my experiences, likes and dislikes, my very human sense of right and wrong," Kevin said. Then he raised his voice to carry and began to weave his way to the front of the group. "Stop at the last door on the left."

Red slowed his step to meet mine. "Kevin's a wise kid."

"He grew up too fast," I said. "That makes for a lot of early wisdom."

If growing up too fast didn't completely fuck you up, it offered hard-earned knowledge. And, sometimes, bitterness about what you lost—or what you never had.

I changed the subject. "You get a read on Faith?"

Red nodded. "She's about seventy-five percent of what she used to be, twenty-five too bright for me to see too deep into."

I pressed my lips into a thin line. "She talks like my kid and walks like my kid."

"But she hasn't said a personal word to you and she hasn't hugged you, and that's not like her."

I nodded.

Kevin had reached the front of the group and come to a halt in front of the last door on the left, which looked like all the other doors. Tall and crafted of oak. Closed. Magically locked. But this one whispered as Kevin touched his palm to the wood.

I couldn't make out the words, only the tone. The living presence of the place had been set to guard this door with everything in its power, and it had done so.

Kevin whispered to the presence in return, again not in a language I understood, but in gratitude. And he asked the presence to open the door.

The magical lock clicked as it unraveled and the oak swung inward to reveal a door in the western red brick wall of a different alley than the one where the bus stood. We stepped onto asphalt and into the puddled light of a security lamp, breathing in the stink of car exhaust and motor oil, along with the perfume of grease and pancakes from a diner down the block. Dance music traveled on a gust of the salt-stained wind.

It took a second for me to orient to the one-story height of the buildings and the crowns of the oaks that lined the far side of the alley.

Kevin had brought us back to the place where we'd entered his city. We'd traveled from Portland to Houston by way of the sulfur-drenched space between worlds known as the In-Between, arriving in front of Malek's place, Snake Bite Tattoo. Kevin had taken us out of Faery and into the human world again, but into the alley behind Snake Bite rather than in front of it.

No one there but us—and a locked metal shed with a blood-red halo the size of an elephant.

"The hell is that?" I asked.

Rude grinned. "That's Rose."

Charlie coughed. "Someone named Rose is locked in the shed?"

"A man-eating motorcycle named Rose," he said.

That was the most ridiculous thing I'd ever heard. "You're shitting me."

"No, dude," he said.

I glanced at Red.

He raised a brow. "Best leave her alone, then."

Rude nodded. "Best."

"There a back door?" I asked.

Rude shook his head and pulled Charlie closer to his chest. "This way."

I pulled my cell from my pocket and dialed Sunday's number.

She answered on the second ring, her voice like running water over smooth stones. "You weren't supposed to call."

"Unless there's an emergency," I said.

"Damn it, Night."

I sighed. "Just listen."

After I'd finished bringing her up to speed, she remained silent. So silent, I wondered whether the line had gone dead.

CHAPTER 2

RUDE LED US around the red brick building, through more pooled light and dense shadow, our steps kicking up scattered dirt and scuffing loose gravel. We wove a path past Beth's yellow Volkswagen, wedged into its home in the side alley, and then across the front of the building to the door. The neon orange sign in the window that read SNAKE BITE TATTOO had been turned off, but the Christmas lights that hung above the sign still glowed with holiday cheer. Kevin unlocked the door to let us in as I hung up with Sunday.

The place smelled like Malek, like time and snakeskin, old paper and fine whisky. The dimmed lights in the waiting area illuminated enough of the room to keep us from tripping over the furniture—two black vinyl sofas, one stuffed beneath the window and one on the other side of a glass coffee table. The only other light shone through the space beneath the closed door of the back room, through which the murmur of lowered voices slipped toward us, too.

I didn't see any special security, nor did I feel any magical presence as I had at the Faery Court or, for that matter, back in Portland at the house that had become my de facto home of late. Maybe the serpent didn't need anything except a nasty reputation to keep his place interloper-free.

After the dark of the night and the low light of the front room, the brightness in back stung my eyes. White walls. White floor clean enough to eat off of. Speakers mounted near the ceiling. Closet in the back, and a small spare room where Malek maybe slept when he needed to. *If* he slept at all. Bathroom in the far left corner. Spartan. Functional.

Malek's musk here smelled stronger, deeper, as if the room were his den.

He and Beth leaned side-by-side against a long counter on the right. They couldn't have looked more unlike each other physically, the serpent and his apprentice—him in his leather, coat still on, and her in her silly red T-shirt dotted with cussing Christmas elves. The counter behind them was covered in neatly arranged tattooing supplies. There was a stainless steel sink, too. And a large box of matches set behind it.

Right. Malek used his poisonous blood in his inks, and it could not be allowed to linger. Rumors circulated about his blood serving as a mystical cure for any number of terrible diseases, but I'd seen it in action. Used by anyone except Malek himself or Beth, his blood killed, serving up only agony. Better to burn a stray bloody paper towel than risk it falling into the wrong hands.

There was one new addition to his family as of a few days ago. Stacy, the young witch who'd done her best to help Faith and who'd anchored our magical presence in Portland when we invaded the Order's compound.

The magic she'd performed for Faith had almost killed her—it would have if Beth hadn't acted quickly to save her life. Beth had only been able to bring Stacy back from the brink because she carried Malek's magic in her blood. The price had been Stacy's humanity, and her freedom.

She'd lived. And she was pissed.

She straddled one of the rolling chairs on the other side of the room, one arm cradling the seat back and the other waving to punctuate whatever she'd been saying to the others. Her halo had turned a shade darker than before, closing in on the deepest indigo of the night sky. Her frizzy blond curls dusted her shoulders. She wore a cobalt-blue cardigan over a white T-shirt, a yellow-and-blue striped broomstick skirt, and matching tights. She'd kicked off her black clogs and pushed them in front of her. A low table and a big chair meant to seat a customer lay between her and Beth and Malek.

She looked up as we walked into the room, words fading from her lips, and met my gaze. A smile lit her face. She scrambled to her feet and rushed to hug me.

She squeezed me tight enough to tweak the stitches near my ribs.

I winced.

"Sorry." She pulled away. "I'm so glad you're here."

I took her by the shoulders. "You all right?"

"I haven't killed anyone yet," she said.

"No forgiveness?" I asked.

She rolled her eyes.

Not anytime soon, in other words.

She stepped back, making room for me to find a place to sit or stand, wrapping her arms around Red as I walked toward the table. Corey and Faith filed in, taking their hugs with joy and a reasonable amount of grace, respectively. They joined Beth and Malek, leaning against the counter. Kevin closed the door behind us, standing guard, as Red made his way over to sit with me and Rude set Charlie down in the big chair.

He knelt beside the kid. "Okay?"

Charlie nodded.

Malek looked at each of us in turn. After a moment, he raised his hands to sign.

This is everyone. What we say here stays here.

"We have people in Portland," I said. "They're in."

They don't know what they're signing up for.

"Doesn't matter," I said.

He held my gaze, his gray eyes filled to the brim with judgment.

"I get it," I said. "You haven't met them. You don't trust them."

He showed me a ghost of a grin.

"I trust them," I said.

His expression told me that he'd hold me responsible if any of them fucked up. I was fine with that. I allowed my own expression to show that, while I granted him the respect due to someone who…was what he was…I wasn't the least bit afraid of him.

Beth stepped forward. "So, there's a new Horseman in play. As we all know, that blows. I've got one more crucial piece of bad news."

Stacy sighed. "We don't need you to pause for dramatic effect."

Beth narrowed her eyes. "We have a report that an archangel's been spotted in the human world." She turned toward me. "In Portland."

Help or hindrance—which would it be? "Michael?"

She shook her head. "Gabriel."

An unknown quantity. The last thing we needed was a wild card. That was exactly how I thought of an angel with that much juice mixing it up in my city with a Horseman already on the loose and the people I loved in his crosshairs.

Kevin folded his arms across his chest. "That's confirmed?"

Beth nodded.

"Shit," Kevin said.

"How did you confirm that?" I asked. "Who do you have reporting to you from Portland?"

"No one there," Kevin said. "We've got someone that Gabriel made —someone who had no magic at all until he showed up and gave it to them. He moves in and out of this world. When he's in, we know because our friend feels it."

"Your friend know what Gabriel's up to in Portland?" I asked.

"More of the same, most likely. Handing out magic to unsuspecting normals."

That was dangerous as hell. This was getting better all the time. "We need to go."

Malek pushed off of the counter, stepping toward the center of the room. *Not yet. I need your blood.*

I narrowed my eyes. My blood allowed me to hold the Angel

without my physical body disintegrating because I descended from Michael. The Order had wanted my blood to power up an Elder being known as the End, who wanted to bring about the destruction of all the worlds. My blood was power.

What did the serpent from the Garden of Eden, whose own poison blood could kill, want with mine?

Charlie won't make it long enough to help you solve the mystery of the third Horseman—or to bring his besieged children through time—without help. None of us can heal Charlie, not even you—not yet. I want to give him, and all of us, a chance. To do that, I need to mark him.

Mark him. Meaning, tattoo him.

My blood won't be enough. You're the one with the archangel's blood, and you carry the only Horseman who has a chance in hell of righting the balance.

Blood magic was dangerous. Spilling your blood as an offering attracted beings that fed off blood—vampiric beings. The key to a person's ancestry and particle makeup lived in the blood, as did the magic they contained. Malek wanted that magic for this operation.

"You planning to use my blood alone?" I asked.

He shook his head.

"Any idea what mixing mine with yours will do, exactly?" I asked. "Side effects?"

No idea at all, he said. *But Stacy assures me she can use her magic to stabilize the mix.*

I met Stacy's gaze. The wrinkles in her forehead didn't look confident.

"How?" I asked.

She thought for a moment. "I'll have to feel my way. Make adjustments as needed."

She was still recovering from her near-death experience and the vast power she'd expended to connect our magic during our battle with the Order. Still getting used to her binding to Malek. She had no business witching anything right now.

I kept that off of my face, but let it settle in my eyes for her alone to see.

She returned the gaze with resignation. We needed her. Therefore, she would do everything in her power to help. Even if it cost her.

Charlie's voice cracked as he spoke softly from the chair. "I'd like to live, please."

In the face of that, I couldn't blame Stacy for overspending her magical bank. And there was no way I would say no, either. But I hadn't come to town with any weapons other than my magic. "I need a clean knife."

Kevin reached beneath his long shirt and pulled a blade from his belt. "Silver?"

I didn't care what it'd been crafted from. "Is it sharp?"

He passed it to me. "Wicked edge. No serpent blood."

I nodded. "Then let's get started."

Malek pointed to the back of his neck, indicating the place on Charlie's body he would tattoo. Although that would be easy to do sitting up for someone not under the influence of a Horseman's soul-deep illness, it would be easier on Charlie if he lay down. Red, Kevin, and I vacated the table, leaving room for Rude to lift Charlie into position.

I headed for the counter in enough time to catch Malek puncturing the tip of his little finger with his own knife, adding exactly three drops of his blood to ink he'd already prepared. He licked the wound, which began to knit itself. Then he wiped the trace amount of blood on the blade with a paper towel and handed it to Beth, who struck a match and burned the paper to ash in the sink.

I raised the knife I held. "How much from me?"

As soon as I asked the question, the Angel answered in my mind—not with words, but with images. I followed them like breadcrumbs, a trail leading me in the general direction I should travel.

Stacy wasn't the only one who would have to feel her way forward. This wasn't an exact science. It was an experiment, one we had a reasonable right to believe would work. Or work enough.

I closed my eyes for a moment, concentrating on the thump of my heart in my chest and everything about it, from the way it pumped oxygen-rich blood through my body and accepted what returned, spent and full of toxins, to the connections forged in love and magic, with my daughter, with Sunday, with all the other people I'd grown to love and called family. The connection that burned brightest, the heart bond with Red, glowed before my inner eye.

He felt the brightness and the heat of it, too. Another heartbeat and I felt him beside me, leaning close enough that I felt his breath against my skin.

"You need me?" he asked.

"I don't know," I said. "I'm winging this."

He braced his feet on the floor, just in case.

My magic rose within me like a geyser, and with it, the bone-deep chill of the grave that marked the Angel's power. I let both fill me until the fine hairs on my arms stood up and the hair on my head began to rise. Until the edges of my skin buzzed electric. Until I could see my own halo, black as the name I'd chosen.

I infused all of the magic we'd brought to the surface with the love I carried inside, with whatever healing something like that might bring. I breathed it in. I breathed it out.

Deft fingers took Kevin's knife from my hand—Malek's. He sliced the skin over my heart, holding a small glass cup beneath the wound to catch the trickle of red that fell. I couldn't see how much blood he'd collected, but I could tell when he'd gathered what was needed. I felt it in my gut a second before the Angel's voice echoed in my head.

Enough.

I met Malek's gray gaze. He pulled the cup away and replaced it with a paper towel, lifting my hand into place to apply pressure to the cut. I watched him pour my blood into the ink and stir. And I watched as the ink grew a halo of its own, black and white. Darkness and bone.

Malek glanced over his shoulder, raising a brow.

I shrugged. We were past the end of the line on the map of the known world here. "It's a living thing."

Beth stepped around him, reaching toward me with her hand outstretched. She wanted the paper towel. I checked the wound on my chest. It'd already closed.

The magic we raised is healing magic, the Angel said.

Not the same kind as some of our friends, but it would do all right for us now—it had already done all right. The cut over my heart wasn't the only wound the magic had healed. The ache over my ribs, where Sunday had sewn me up a handful of days ago, was also gone.

I handed Beth the paper. She took it back to the sink and, as she'd done with the towel stained with Malek's blood, burned it to ash.

"Can't be too careful," she said.

An understatement.

Red threaded his fingers through mine, leading me back toward the table where Charlie lay. As we passed one of the empty rolling chairs, I hooked my foot around the base and steered it toward the head of the table, sinking down near Charlie's face. He looked so piti-ful, I lifted my hand to tousle his hair.

Stacy wheeled over and settled beside me, near enough to lay hands on Charlie as well. She settled her weight in the chair and set her stocking feet flat on the floor, preparing to do whatever Charlie needed.

Malek cleaned the back of the kid's neck, then went to work free-hand, the buzz of the tattoo gun like angry bees.

Charlie's eyes widened at the first touch of the needle. A moment later, he squeezed them shut. He reached for my hand and squeezed that, too. The greenish cast to his halo began to fade as the tattoo took shape—an infinity symbol.

Stacy pushed out of her chair and laid hands on the small of Char-lie's back. The green disappeared in a flash, and a healthy brick-red filled in most of the empty space, with the magic Stacy offered and the magic of the tattoo slipping into the cracks between the red like mortar.

The pressure Charlie applied to my fingers let up a little.

Red whistled softly. "The sickness is still woven into his soul, but it's not making any more inroads. It looks frozen in place."

A heartbeat later, Malek set down the tattoo gun. Charlie passed out.

I sucked in a breath, expecting his magic to take over the way Sunday had described. Knock the kid out, and he slipped into the timestream, traveling across days or months or years to a when and where he chose, or one chosen for him. The trauma activated his magic.

He didn't vanish.

No time traveling, just a kid passed out from the trauma of a Horseman striking him soul-sick, a witch's healing, and a god inking him with the mixture of our blood.

I looked at Malek as he cleaned and bandaged the tattoo with plastic wrap. "He stable?"

Malek nodded, stripping the gloves from his hands. *Now for the price.*

"Money?" I didn't have any spare cash to part with. No one here looked like they did.

Magical, Malek said. *It's Charlie's to pay, not yours or anyone else's.*

"You didn't tell Charlie before you inked him," I said.

His only other choice was dying right now. Instead, he'll die later.

"How much later?" I asked.

Once his mission is done.

Not this mission. *His* mission. That was a much more personal thing. Something only Charlie and the powers that watched over him could know. My heart grieved for him.

Faith stepped in before I could answer, the fingers of one hand wrapped around my hourglass pendant at the hollow of her throat. "That's terrible."

He swiveled his seat in her direction. *Some things we choose, and some choose us. We become responsible to those things. Charlie has a job to do. He wants to do it. Let him.*

She let go of the pendant, her hands curling into fists at her sides. "But he's just a kid."

A kid younger than herself, at an age she remembered all too well. Who, if Malek was right, wouldn't live long enough to have much of a life.

We all sacrifice, Malek said.

Faith's words came out a whisper. "For what?"

For everyone else, Malek said. *For the people lucky enough to be clueless about other worlds and magic, and how close they come over and over again to being snuffed out like a candle flame. We're fighting so they can have a chance to live.*

"What about us?" she asked.

Malek mirrored the question back to her. *What about us?*

She breathed in his words, turning them over in her heart. Then she spun on her heel and stomped out of the room. A moment later, the front door opened with a single squeak of its hinges, then slammed shut.

Everyone stared after her except Malek, who continued cleaning up.

Kevin and Rude, with understanding and empathy washing across their faces. Stacy, with sadness in her eyes. Red, with his teeth clenched. Heartbreak flowed off of him in waves, and I felt it hard because of the bond.

Corey stood with her mouth open, shifting her weight from one foot to the other. Her eyes welled. She blinked her tears away and pressed the heels of her beringed hands to her forehead. She wore her desire to go after Faith on her sleeve. It warred with fear visible in the quivering downturn of her mouth.

Corey was no coward. She'd proven that in spades. She was just sixteen, and two months ago she'd been as sheltered as a magical child could be.

What could she say to Faith? Malek had spoken a hard truth without an ounce of sugarcoating. He had no investment in any of us as people. We were powers, and we'd committed first to keeping ourselves alive and then to helping others make it through their own hell.

The stakes kept rising. There was no way this fight would end well for everyone.

We weren't going to kick Malek to the curb for being what he was. We needed him, and he needed us.

As I pushed to my feet, he glanced up at me. I met his gaze.

He didn't raise his hands or mouth platitudes or take my measure yet again. He simply looked at me. We were what we were.

I stepped around him, brushing past Corey closely enough to lay a hand on her shoulder.

"It's all right," I said. "I've got this."

She froze beneath my touch. I felt anger ignite in her the way it had before with me where Faith was concerned. I saw it in the color of her cheeks, approaching the fire-engine red of her hair.

Before it could explode from her mouth, Beth swung an arm around her shoulders, turning Corey away from me and from Malek, walking her toward the back corner of the room.

If anyone could talk Corey down right now, Beth could. Beth understood her boss. She'd been through so much herself, her mortality stripped away in an instant because she'd come to the attention of the wrong local god. To save her, Malek had changed her utterly. Beth knew a little of what Faith was going through.

I left the brightly lit room, the unconscious time traveler, and the crew of powers behind, stepping into the darkened waiting area with its glass-topped table and magazines—the façade that allowed people who entered to pretend that Snake Bite Tattoo was like any other tattoo place in the world, that its proprietor was there to help them express on the outside what mattered to them on the inside.

It was so much more than that.

I followed Faith into the night.

CHAPTER 3

FAITH HAD FLED only ten feet or so. I found her out front, leaning against the wall with her arms folded across her chest. The salty breeze lifted her dark hair from her shoulders, tossing it into a tangle in front of her mouth. She didn't glance my way. She didn't say a word. Just stared at the curve of Westheimer Road and the single white pickup that rolled past, its closed windows barely containing the thumping bass of the hip-hop blasting from its speakers.

Across the way, the leather bar had lowered the volume of its dance music. Only a couple of motorcycles graced the parking lot. I let my power rise, listening for unexpected movements or vibrations, feeling for unexpected magic. Nothing at the moment.

Beth had thrown down a brief explanation about the spell placed on the sidewalk here—how it should prevent magical tracking once we left the place. And there was Malek and his reputation to consider. Good to know the shop had some protections.

And Faith was a god with the power to vaporize anyone stupid enough to attack her, but she was also an upset seventeen-year-old girl trying to figure out how to be a grown-ass young woman. That made her vulnerable.

Pissed and uncomfortable as she was, at least she had the good sense to stand with her back to a wall.

I leaned against the brick beside her. I'd been this close to her at the Faery court, but she hadn't so much as acknowledged my nearness. We'd been with people then, two of them strangers. Now we were alone—the way we'd been for most of our time together. Two against the world.

The fine hairs on my arms pricked the way they had in the alley out back with its man-eating magical motorcycle spelled into a shed. Here, it wasn't about magic. Here, it was about love and trust.

Before I could open my mouth, she shook her head. "Don't say it, Night."

I waited a breath. "What do you think I'm about to say?"

"That Malek is right and I'm dumb."

"It's dumb to think I was gonna say any of that."

She gave me the side-eye. "I don't want him to be right."

"No one wants him to be right," I said. "What he said is fucking bleak."

She looked away, as if she didn't want me to see her face.

"It's not right," I said. "But there's truth to it."

"I don't get it. Like I said, dumb."

I shook my head. Even if she couldn't see my head move, she felt it. "When the Awakened came alive inside you, do you remember what you told me?"

She didn't answer.

"You said you were still in there and that you'd be all right. You said that you had to go because you had to gather the magical children and keep them safe. Remember?"

A grudging nod.

"How did that feel?" I asked.

"I had to go, but I didn't want to. I knew I was needed, and that I would do whatever it took to make sure the kids I was supposed to protect were safe. But it tore me away from my life."

"It's complicated," I said.

"Yeah. But Malek's not saying it's complicated. He's saying I shouldn't want a life and that I'm wrong for feeling sad about every-thing that's changed—about how I've changed."

"Maybe," I said.

"What's maybe about it, Night?"

I could've said a lot of things—how one of the only things we could count on was that things change, how a single day's experiences could change a person overnight. Those things were true, but they wouldn't help my kid. "Maybe is I don't want to try climbing inside Malek's head to figure out what he meant."

"He's creepy as fuck," she said.

"He really is." I pushed off the wall, turning toward her. "I can only tell you how I took what he said. You want to know?"

She nodded once.

I took a deep breath. "We have to get right with what we've lost and what we've got. We have to figure out how to handle our changes and what we're willing to fight for—how far we're willing to go for ourselves and for other people, other worlds. That's our stuff to do, and we have to do it, because what's happening is bigger than us, and it's happening now."

She met my gaze, brow furrowed. "You're not just talking about me. You're talking about yourself, too."

Not by design. But Faith wasn't the only one facing life-altering changes. "I'm growing goddamn wings."

"The Angel," she said.

"The Angel. Everything comes back to that guy."

That earned me the ghost of a grin that faded quickly. "Is he on your side?"

The question crashed through me like a storm-tossed wave. I took my time answering. "I don't know. He's done things or agreed to things that I needed. I don't know whether he's doing them because he's on my side, or because helping me will make me more likely to help him. Does that make sense?"

She let her hands fall to her sides. "You scratch my back, I'll scratch yours?"

"Something like that."

"There's something else," she said.

Something else I wasn't saying? I remembered she hadn't been there for the lead-up to infiltrating the Order.

"He's more powerful than I am," I said.

"But you overpowered him before. You trapped him in your mind."

"He's more powerful now. Maybe it's because he's got a human vessel. Maybe it's because some part of him is waking up, like the god inside of you. Brass tacks, he can overpower me when he wants to. Take control."

She blinked at me. "What happened when he did?"

"He showed me a piece of my past," I said. "My training with the Order scrambled some of my memories a little."

She raised a brow.

"Okay, a lot," I said. "The Angel showed me my *abuelita*. He showed me more of who I was, who I am. He helped me figure out how to take on the Order—combining all of our magic to go up against the End."

"Doesn't sound bad," she said. "Sounds like it worked out."

"It did," I said. "The Angel helped save a lot of those kids you're gathering. I'm so grateful for that, I don't have words. And every single time the Angel and I combine our most powerful magic, I become less of what I was—a magical human—and more of something else."

She mulled that over. "So how do you keep doing that, knowing what it's doing to you?"

"I don't know that either," I said. "I only know that I'm in the fight and I'm not backing down. I'm taking it one choice at a time."

She sprinkled on the sarcasm. "And here I thought you were coming out here to coddle me and give me an easy answer."

I cracked a smile. "Since when?"

Her face opened up, shining with a sea change of emotion. "I missed you."

I breathed in her words, holding tight to them. "I missed you, too, Faith."

"Thanks for bringing Corey," she said.

"As if I could stop her from coming."

For a second, I thought she'd say something about how much she loved Corey—Corey certainly loved the hell out her. But instead, she worried at her lip. "How are the others?"

The others were the two remaining members of their fearsome foursome. They'd managed to find each other after Faith and I settled in Portland and had become close fast. Everything that had happened since had only drawn them closer.

"Ben and Jess are good. They were worried about you. Sunday will have told them by now that we found you."

She sighed relief. And stepped closer to me.

I opened my arms. She rushed into them, pulling me close. Her hands found the small bulges in the back of my shirt—the nubs of my wings.

"Whoa," she said.

"I told you."

"There's a difference between hearing it and feeling it. Black feathers?"

"Yes," I said.

She pulled away slowly and looked me in the eye. "We should go back in."

"You gonna be okay with Malek?"

"No," she said. "Does it matter?"

I brushed a wayward strand of hair from her face. "Let me know if you think it should."

She nodded. "Deal."

I let her lead the way back into Snake Bite, taking the time to do another magical and sense sweep of the sidewalk and the street.

Something was off.

I felt a pull in my belly—an attraction—as if I were one magnet drawn toward another. Or a compass needle, drawn toward true north. I turned toward the pull.

My gaze landed on a female with pigtails thirty or so yards away on the other side of the street, leaning against the sign pole in front of a convenience store. I'd never seen her before, but I knew who she was. I knew it in my bones, the way I knew what love was, what family was for. That girl was family to me, but of a kind I'd never known before. A kind I had no desire to know.

She vanished as I watched. The breeze brought a whiff of sulfur—a dead giveaway that she'd stepped into the space between the worlds, the In-Between.

I waited a moment to see whether she'd come back, but the spot under the sign remained empty.

Something felt off about my body. It took me a moment to realize that I was shaking.

I took a deep breath, counting to four, held my breath for a similar count, then exhaled to a count of six. I did that three times, letting the longer outbreath calm my nerves.

She's your sister, the Angel said.

Another Horseman. Or Horsewoman. Famine.

Beth had told me about her. She and Beth had some kind of entwined destiny. Mortal enemies.

The last thing we needed was another Horseman on the scene. Two was more than fucking enough, thanks very much.

The Angel's wings fluttered inside me, the tips brushing against my rib cage. Always a sign that I should pay attention. That I should think.

Two more Horsemen. Plus me. Made three.

I shivered.

What does it mean? I asked.

Too soon to tell, the Angel said.

How could it be too soon? Wasn't there some kind of lore about it? The Bible certainly had things to say about how the world would end.

Aren't you supposed to know this? I asked.

It's different every time, he said.

Every. Time?

The world ends over and over again. Each new age. Each life-ending catastrophe. Each and every death.

A bunch of riddles. Great. *You picked a great time to go philosophical on me.*

You'll understand soon enough.

I don't think you understand the meaning of 'soon enough,' I said.

The Angel was silent.

I sighed.

Stepping into Snake Bite again, I locked the door behind me and marched into the back room, where Faith had settled against the counter beside Corey once more. Stacy, Kevin, and Rude talked amongst themselves, while Red stood with his hands on his hips near the table where Charlie slept. Malek and Beth had segregated themselves in the shadowed back corner, the serpent blank-faced while Beth laid into him with whispers and emphatic gestures.

"Famine was here," I said.

Every one of them turned toward me.

"Down the street," I said. "Watching Faith and me. She disappeared after I noticed."

Beth went around Malek, moving into the light. The whites of her eyes looked a little bloodshot. "This is because of you. Or because of Charlie—what Pestilence did to him. I'm guessing she can feel you."

"I certainly felt her before I saw her."

"That could come in handy," Beth said.

"No doubt." I'd use it for whatever advantage I could gain. "What's going on in here?"

Beth shrugged. "Malek and I are having a conversation about allocation of resources."

"Resources?"

"People," she said. "We need to figure out who's staying here and who's going to Portland."

"What's he saying that you don't like?" I asked.

She sighed. "I don't want to leave again so soon. I might be needed here. He says I should go with you."

Some small part of me—the wishful thinking part—hoped that Faith would come with us. I wanted more time with her. But her place was with the kids, at least for now. And Corey belonged with Faith

This raised parental problems, of course. It raised school problems, too. The kids were on Christmas vacation right now, but that would come to an end soon. Truancy laws wouldn't wait on the impending Apocalypse.

We'd deal with it. One problem at a time.

Meanwhile, Beth was a strong ally. She got shit done. She was a connection to Malek if we needed him.

"He's right," I said.

She scowled.

I held her gaze.

After a second, she blew out the breath she'd been holding. "Stacy's in no shape to travel, or she could go."

Stacy glared from her spot at the foot of the table. "Stacy's sitting right here."

Beth waved her off. "And Kevin can't go. He's key to the bus defense."

Of course he was. The bus was located in Faery. He was the Faery King. Of the folks assembled in this room, that left Rude. He had some serious magical juice. We could use him, even if I didn't like him all that much. I looked his way.

"Dude, I have obligations," he said. "I have a sworn duty to protect the city."

Beth rolled her eyes. "You're not a superhero, Rudolph."

"Your mileage may vary, Elizabeth," he said. "I thought my role here was clear."

Malek looked at Beth. He didn't raise his hands to sign. He didn't need to. She got his message loud and clear.

She was going whether she wanted to or not.

Beth gritted her teeth, but she left off with the objections.

"It's settled, then," I said. "We leave as soon as Charlie's up. I'm not taking him through the In-Between while he's unconscious. Especially if Famine is watching."

"Good call," Beth said.

I asked a question of Malek. "How long 'til he wakes?"

Couple of hours, max, he said.

"What time is it now?" I asked.

Rude thumped his watch with his index finger. "Just after five."

Oh-dark-thirty. I rubbed my eyes. "I need food, coffee, and twenty minutes of shut-eye."

Beth nodded in sympathy. "I can do two out of three. Better if I pick up something to go. Anyone want to come with?"

Hands went up: everyone except Kevin, Malek, and me. I couldn't blame them. The shop had its merits, but such a small space filled with so many people—and so much power—could start to feel confining. That, on top of lack of sleep and the aforementioned food and coffee, made people punchy, soon after which people would get fidgety and pace and say things they didn't mean.

If Famine was out there, well, she was out there. She'd have to be stupid to attack the group. And anyway, Beth notwithstanding, what she seemed to want intended to stay right here.

I didn't know why. It was just a feeling, and I trusted it.

Red looked at Faith and Corey, then at me, making his intention clear. He'd keep an eye on our girls whether or not they needed it. That meant everything. I sent him a well of gratitude through the heart link.

He planted a kiss on my mouth on his way out the door. The salt taste of him lingered on my lips as the last of the magical breakfast train filed out into the pre-dawn. Their footfalls faded, leaving only silence inside.

Kevin slid his hands into his pockets. "So. What do we need to talk about?"

Malek shrugged and looked at me.

Funny, I thought he would be the one to start. I had no idea what we should talk about—and why that conversation should be private, among the three of us. My gut feeling provided a clue.

Famine. But not just her.

"I'm here, with the Angel of Death," I said. "So is Famine. And Pestilence is looking for a human vessel. We're missing one Horseman: War."

Kevin ticked off the questions I'd raised. "Who will Pestilence and

War take as human vessels? What kind of magic will their vessels have, and how will it combine with the Horsemen's? What side will they fall on—our side, the side of life, or the End's side, obliteration?"

Malek signed. *How will having more Horsemen in the human world change the world?*

With that kind of power walking around, change was inevitable. I asked the last question, the one neither of them had spoken. "When all four Horsemen are here in the world, does that start something that can't be stopped?"

"The big-A Apocalypse?" Kevin asked.

I nodded.

"What does the Angel say?"

"A lot of nothing," I said. "Malek?"

He was the oldest one here—or at least he was a contemporary of the Angel. Since-the-beginning-of-time old.

You've probably figured out by now—there's no book source that can be trusted, he said.

"Yeah, I got that."

There is lore, but it's vague.

"What—philosophy? Myth? Metaphors?" I asked.

Malek flashed a wry grin.

"The Angel said that the world has ended before. That it ends all the time, every day."

Malek cocked his head. *The big one was the flood. Water.*

Kevin pulled his hands from his pockets, brushing his overgrown hair back from his face. "Next one, according to the lore, is supposed be fire."

"End of the world by fire," I said.

"That's the one," he said.

"Sounds unpleasant."

Kevin raised a brow. "So, the Four Horsemen. Let's circle back to that."

We should try to prevent all of the Horsemen from becoming embodied in this world, Malek said.

"Stop Pestilence," I said. "Stop War."

It's something, he said.

Something. As if the best we could hope for was handling what was thrown our way, one step at a time. "You really don't know any more than the rest of us, do you?"

Malek pressed his lips together. *I know the End.*

From his expression, he didn't mean figuratively. "How?"

He mulled how to answer. *This information doesn't leave the room. Not yet.*

Kevin opened his mouth to agree, but I rolled over him.

"I don't know whether I can agree to that," I said. "I'm going to fight a Horseman and the Powers know what else with people I love and trust who might need your information to save a life or come out on top. I need a reason."

The information could be used against me, he said.

As if we didn't all have those kinds of problems. Also, after what he'd said to Faith, I couldn't let that stand. "You're giving my kid shit for wondering what her human place in all of this is—whether she's gonna be able to survive and whether she can live with herself—and that's your reason?"

He ignored what I said and came back with a nice non sequitur. *I'm not invulnerable.*

I stared at him. I took in his words—and their meaning. Malek was telling me he could be hurt or maybe even killed. A god cursed into human form who'd walked the earth from its beginning.

I hadn't thought about it much, but it seemed to me that whoever had done that to him, it'd been the worst they could do. The worst that could be done to Malek, period.

That he was willing to tell me at all—a stranger with a Horseman inside of her—proved that he would do anything to keep the worlds, and the people in them, alive. If I respected that, I had to agree to his terms.

"Okay," I said.

He closed the distance between us, and Kevin pushed away from the table to join us. I met Kevin's gaze, noting how goddamn young he was, how much power he held and the extraordinary grace with which he handled it. How much Malek trusted him to include him in this conversation.

I looked at Malek, into his ancient gray eyes. "Did the End curse you?" I asked.

It's how he did it that's important, Malek said.

We waited while Malek chose the rest of his words.

There were no gods in any of the worlds except *the worlds,* he said.

"The worlds themselves—the earth and wind and light and stars—are gods," Kevin said.

A statement, not a question. That was how Kevin saw things. How the *Faery King* saw them.

Malek nodded. *The End was the only other being in existence at that time. Maybe he didn't like the competition. I've spent millennia wondering, but in the end it doesn't matter. He created me from the dust and light of the human world and imbued me with magic poisonous to that world. He taught me to hate. He fed me cruelty. He gave me fear to drink, and clothed me in its cousin, arrogance. All for the purpose of destroying the worlds and every creature within them. I lived a long time before the first humans were born. I learned everything there was to learn. I knew everything there was to know. I'd been bred for one thing, and one thing only. I knew my time had come around when I first laid eyes on Eve.*

Not quite the creation story I'd heard growing up, but then nothing had ever really been as I'd expected. "Eve. She's real?"

She is, he said. *You know what it is to fall in love? To fall irrevocably?*

I thought of Sunday, whom I still loved. And Red. And our heart link. "Yes."

Then you know what happened when I first saw Eve. What happened after that—I did what I was made to do. I tempted Eve because it was the reason for my existence, who I was in my heart and soul—it was a tragedy. I broke both our hearts, and after that I turned my back on my creator.

He had me cursed then.

"Wait," I said. "He didn't curse you himself?"

Malek shook his head. *He gathered together the beings that were destined to be present at the end of the worlds, and he forced them to do it. He had more power than they did at the time, and they had no choice.*

The beings destined to be present at the end of the worlds.

The Angel's wings fluttered inside my chest.

"The Horsemen," I said.

The Horsemen, he replied. *I didn't see them again, not in all the years I've walked the earth in this form, until Famine moved against my apprentice.*

My legs wanted to give way. I backed into the counter, leaning against it for support.

Events came together in my mind like pieces of a jigsaw puzzle, colors and shapes finally making sense. I put myself in Malek's shoes and I knew.

He'd sent Beth to Portland with Stacy not just to serve as a deterrent or bodyguard against forces that might attack the witch, but because of me. He'd wanted a glimpse of the Angel of Death, one of the beings who'd cursed him. He wanted to know who I was, where I stood, which side I was on. Which side the Angel had taken. All of that, down to how familiar he seemed when I'd first seen him in the alley.

"Who would use that information against you?" I asked.

The Horsemen cursed me individually, one after the other—they did not use their collective might, he said. *It was the one thing they could do to exert their will under the circumstances.*

The Horsemen. Two walking in the human world, two on deck.

Kevin cleared his throat. "If they had cursed you collectively?"

Malek shrugged.

In other words, he didn't know, but it would be bad. Seriously bad.

However I felt about the guy—I hadn't yet made up my mind—I knew one thing. He was one of the most valuable allies we had. We couldn't afford to lose him.

This isn't about me, he said. *Not entirely.*

I understood. Malek wasn't asking me to prevent Pestilence from taking a vessel to save his own ass, although that would be his preferred side effect. He was telling me that he believed the Horse-men, when gathered together, were more powerful than he was.

I didn't even know how to wrap my mind around that. Not in the ways that mattered most.

The Angel's wings fluttered around my heart.

CHAPTER 4

I INHALED DEEP and exhaled a shuddering breath. The air in the spotless back room of Snake Bite Tattoo tasted of secrets. The counter behind me felt unforgiving, the edge biting into the small of my back, the silence among Malek, Kevin, and me a living thing.

Any minute, the mob of loved ones would arrive bearing breakfast and coffee. I had a long way to go to take in everything Malek had said—the implications for him, for me, for the fight. Each second felt precious.

Malek studied me, his gray eyes measuring once again. He'd asked Kevin and me to hold his words close, and I would honor that promise even if I wanted nothing more than to talk over every nuance with Red or Sunday.

He saw it in my face and relaxed, the sink of his shoulders so slight, I'd have missed it if I'd blinked.

"You're not just asking for my discretion," I said. "You're asking for my help."

You're in a position to do so, he signed.

"I don't have control over the Angel."

Kevin cocked his head. His white-feathered wings ruffled. "He takes over?"

"When he wants or needs to," I said.

"Wants?" he asked.

"A couple of days ago, the Angel took control of my mind, pushing me into a repressed memory of my *abuelita* and me at the beach in Galveston, talking about the stars in the sky and who I was—my reason for being—as a hurricane approached. He wanted me to see it, to pick up on information that would help us march into the Order and win the day in a magical battle against the End."

Kevin whistled. "Damn."

"He's taken control to save my life, too," I said. "He picked up my magically shredded remains and put me back together."

Any sense of control you feel is at his sufferance, Malek said.

"In one sense, yes."

What's the other?

"He mostly keeps his thoughts to himself, and he doesn't run my day-to-day," I said.

Kevin mulled that over. "But he feels close. As if he's a part of you. And you're growing those wings."

I nodded.

He sighed.

"What?" I asked.

"Symbiosis," he said.

I'd only ever heard that term applied scientifically. Then again, I tended to view magic as a craft and a science—and so much of what we now called science, humans once upon a time thought of as magic.

Symbiosis: two different beings living together, dependent on each other. That characterization of my relationship with the Angel stuck in my craw. I didn't want to depend on him. I wanted him to be a temporary visitor.

The wings coming in at my shoulder blades said otherwise.

"Just calling it like I see it," Kevin said.

I met his gaze. His brown, human eyes. The power that radiated. "Are you talking about it objectively, or from experience?"

His lips curved. "Door number two."

"Who's your Angel?" I asked.

"The former Faery Queen." He tapped his temple with an index finger. "She lives in here. Thoughts, feelings, magical know-how. Ancestral knowledge of the fae—which I could not rule without, by the way. She sees and hears and knows everything I think and feel and do, even if she doesn't focus her attention on it at the time. It's unnerving and uncomfortable as hell, especially for an introvert. Or at least that's what I was before I became what I am now."

"It doesn't drive you out of your mind?" I asked.

"No," he said. "It just takes a lot of getting used to. I'm still getting used to it, actually. It's only been a handful of months."

"You're handling it with remarkable grace," I said.

His cheeks flushed. He talked past the embarrassment at the compliment. "It was my choice. I'd do it again."

The choices I'd made to leave the Order, to spare Faith's life and take her with me, to raise her—I'd do it all again. I'd taken on the Angel to save her, first trapping him in my mind and then collaborating with him again and again once he'd escaped his cage. He'd stayed with me. I'd made no move to exorcise him. Not exactly the framework for a symbiotic relationship, but there it was.

"I know what you mean," I said. "If I have no control over the Angel, that means I have no control over what he may or may not choose to do if the remaining Horsemen show up and you're there."

Malek flashed a grin that vanished just as fast. *You may have more power than you think.*

I hoped that was true. "I'll keep it in mind."

Stop Pestilence from taking a vessel, he said.

"If I can do it, it'll be done," I said.

Kevin glanced toward the door. "Our people are almost here."

I listened, but didn't hear what he did. "How can you tell?"

"I'm fae. Remember, we shape everything in our realm before it rises into the human world and becomes what you call reality. I marked their leaving before they did it, and I feel their return before it happens."

"Something that small? That insignificant?" I asked.

"There's nothing about any of them that I'd call insignificant," he said. "Usually, I wouldn't be paying attention to something so trivial as a bunch of people heading out to pick up breakfast. But these people, I'm watching."

"And Famine's watching," I said. "And who knows who else."

He nodded.

Across the room, on the table, Charlie groaned.

I looked at Malek. "How much of that did our time traveler hear?"

None of it, he said.

He seemed very sure. It was his secret. Let him worry about Charlie keeping it if need be.

"You okay over there?" I asked.

Charlie pushed up on his elbows, blinking. "What happened? Is it over?"

"The ink, yes. The healing, yes. The problem, no."

He sighed, part relief and part exasperation. "We're leaving soon?"

"Yep," I said. "Soon."

Kevin stepped back, breaking up our huddle.

The front door opened. In swarmed the group, engaged in at least three conversations, and bringing with them the mouth-watering scent of coffee and breakfast burritos.

Red met my gaze, his lips curving into a smile. A moment later, his grin faltered.

Hard enough to hide the discomfort that swirled around my heart from his linked heart, but harder still when his magic allowed him to see through any barriers I might erect, all the way to my soul.

He read the room, too, like the perceptive man he was. He didn't say a word. He just kept a weather eye on me while pretending to watch Beth share out the breakfast, along with crumpled handfuls of paper napkins.

"I thought y'all were going to the diner," I said.

He shook his head. "I thought so, too, but there's a guy who sells these out of a hot pack on the corner two blocks further down."

"You check him?" I asked.

Not just for bad intent, but for the presence of magic as well. Our enemies came in all flavors, including the faction of the Order comprised of magical chameleons—people whose magic had been reworked like iron in a forge, remaking them into beings who could change their appearance and impersonate someone else's magic. Checking for authenticity was starting to become second nature, but it wasn't entirely. Not yet. We couldn't afford to let our guard down.

"What do you take me for?" Red handed me my very large, steaming cup with a grin.

"A god." I took a sip of my coffee and groaned with pleasure, forgetting momentarily that the fate of the worlds rested in our hands —or that Malek's fate might rest in mine.

"Smart woman."

I tried.

I watched Beth as she ate—the way her body settled into the notion that she'd be headed back to Portland with us. By the time she finished her burrito, she'd dropped a glop of molten cheddar on her profane Christmas shirt and grown a measure of peace and resolve.

I had no idea whether she knew the info her boss shared with Kevin and me, and I couldn't ask her about it since I'd agreed not to share. But Malek's insistence that she come with us struck me as him keeping a closer eye on us—on me—than he'd initially intended to.

I didn't need a babysitter. Or a spy.

Or maybe she feared something in particular. I couldn't imagine what the serpent's apprentice would fear, but anything was possible.

I stuffed down the rest of my breakfast and wiped my hands with my wad of napkins. "All right. Twenty minutes, then wheels up."

That touched off a scramble to eat and drink faster and gather any needed items before we opened a door into the In-Between. Kevin took his cue to leave, grabbing me by the sleeve as he headed for the door. I followed him.

He spoke low, for only the two of us to hear. "Be careful with Beth."

"It's not my first time working with her," I said.

"She's impulsive," he said.

"Her impulses have been good so far," I said. "She's also steady under fire."

"She bites off more than she can chew. She still has a curiosity problem, even after everything she's been through."

I held up a hand. "Okay. Point taken."

"Call if you need me," he said.

"No cell signal in Faery."

"Don't use your cell," he said. "Ask a crow."

That sparked a memory that'd stuck with me—of traveling through the In-Between with Beth, and her pointing out a crow in an oak tree there. She'd said the crow functioned as a messenger.

"We've got plenty of those in Portland," I said.

He nodded. "Don't hesitate."

Two offers of help in less than a minute from someone who saw the future before it happened. "You see something coming that I should know about?"

He shook his head. "No. It's more of a feeling. Something's coming. The air feels full, like we're inside a balloon and someone's filling it up. You can't do that forever."

Eventually, the thin rubber would break under the pressure. I mimicked the impending explosion with my hands.

"Yeah," he said. "Anyway, I have a soft spot for people like us."

"Like us?" We couldn't be less alike.

He touched his index finger to his temple. "Those of us with voices in our heads."

Humans—or former humans—who carried powerful magical beings within. He had me there.

"I'll call if I need you," I said. "Take care of yourself, Kevin."

"You, too, Night."

He slipped out into the morning light. A heartbeat later, he sank through the cracked concrete of the sidewalk into the earth below.

There weren't any shouts of alarm. No one came running. So,

either no one saw Kevin disappear into the ground, or people around here had gotten used to seeing some pretty incredible shit.

I felt Red before I heard his footsteps—the grass and earth of his magic wrapped around me a full second before his arms circled my waist.

"Can you tell me what happened while we were gone?" he asked.

"Malek, Kevin, and I had a conversation."

"About?"

I shook my head.

"Not now?"

"Not at all," I said. "Malek swore us to secrecy."

He took that in. "The world's not ending tomorrow, is it?"

"Not that I know of."

"Good news." He leaned closer, planting a kiss on my cheek. "It's almost time."

To head home. Just the two of us—without Faith or Corey. But with Beth and Charlie Nobody.

"Crappy trade," I said. "Those two for our girls."

"I can't disagree," he said.

Behind us, Faith cleared her throat. I glanced over my shoulder, and Red's, to find her leaning against the doorframe, halfway in and halfway out of the back room. Corey stood beside her.

"Are we interrupting?" Faith asked.

Red pulled away. "Nope."

He headed toward Corey, taking her hand in his and drawing her a few feet away. I caught the first few words of their conversation before I focused on Faith—something about Corey calling her parents and Red handling the rest.

I didn't know how he planned to do that, exactly.

It occurred to me that I had no idea what Corey's parents knew about her extracurricular activities. They'd have to know about her magic. Most of the time, magic manifested when kids were very young, and no small child would be able to keep their mouth shut about seeing and talking with ghosts.

There was so much I didn't know about the teenagers in my

adopted family. So much I hadn't thought about because there'd been no time to think.

I met Faith's gaze, the gold and silver of her halo dazzling.

She reached up and smoothed my forehead with her fingers. "Worry lines."

"Plenty to worry about," I said.

"It won't help," she said.

She was right. Making a plan helped. Taking action helped. "You'll be here with Malek and Stacy, or in Faery with Kevin?"

"Unless there's another magical kid to pick up and bring here."

"You won't be going by yourself," I said.

"Corey will be with me. I get the feeling that, even if I didn't want her to come with—even if I left her here—she'd find a way to find me."

"Listen to that feeling," I said. "It's a true one. You watch out for each other."

She nodded. "You, too."

I wrapped my arms around her. She hugged me back.

"I love you," I said.

She squeezed me harder. "Love you, too."

When she drew back, her eyes seemed suspiciously wet. "Stacy's opening the door for you now."

As far as I knew, Stacy was still in the back room. "Inside the shop?"

"Better than outside if Famine's watching," Faith said.

I had to agree. But opening a door to another world inside Malek's place—creating a hole in Malek's defenses—opened him up to attack. I cocked my head toward the back room as invitation for Faith to follow, then headed that direction.

One minute, the air smelled and tasted of whatever the floor had been cleaned with, and the lingering undercurrent of glass cleaner mixed with worn vinyl and cologne ads inside the magazines on the lobby table. The next, a tinge of sulfur permeated the air, growing in strength and obnoxiousness. I wrinkled my nose.

The door Stacy had opened to the In-Between glowed around the edges, the interior dark as dusk, just before the sun went to ground.

The smell had become a stench. Rude watched the open door with care.

Malek watched, too, with no tension in his body at all. Everything a potential intruder needed to know showed on the serpent's face—a willingness to kill, or at the very least maim, anything or anyone who tried to walk through the door into his domain.

Beth stood beside him, a backpack stuffed to the gills slung over one shoulder and a jade knife in hand. The blade had been gifted to her, and she'd drawn her own blood with it—her blood that contained a microcosm of the poison that Malek's did and was for all purposes just as deadly.

No one on the other side tested the door.

There was nothing left but for those of us who were going to Portland to walk through it.

I hugged Stacy goodbye, and planted a kiss on the crown of Corey's head. I squeezed Faith's hand. She held on until the last possible moment.

Malek nodded at me. He didn't bother to sign. There was nothing left to say.

I let my magic rise within me until it filled me, stretching to the edges of my skin. Red fell in behind me, his heart linked to mine and his soul-seeing magic at the ready. With a stable, if shaky, Charlie behind him and Beth bringing up the rear, we stepped from the human realm into the In-Between.

I held my breath and shut my eyes tightly against searing heat that singed the ends of my hair and lashes, and reddened every inch of my exposed skin. The air cooled as quickly as it'd heated. I punched that breath out of my body and sucked air as my feet hit the ground, every fine hair on my arms and at the back of my neck acting as an antenna, scanning for any vibration that foreshadowed an attack. I sent my magic out to every side, searching.

Nothing.

There was nothing here except a lonely asphalt road lined to our left by mean-looking oak trees that marked one border of the In-Between. I couldn't see past the road on the other side. The sulfur-drenched air and everything it touched had a yellowish, twilit cast to it. It seemed extra thick on our right, like magical smog.

I called over my shoulder. "Beth, is this the same part of the In-Between we've walked before?"

"Don't think so," she said. "Wait. Yeah. That stand of oaks is the same."

If that was true, then in place of the smog there should've been rows of huts. "You think the buildings are still there?"

Beth took her time answering. "I don't know, but I don't think we should try to find out."

"You think it's something specific?" Red asked.

"It's a feeling," she said.

Red sighed. "About now, I'm thinking about the Horsemen—one more in the world, one who makes people sick. Can he make places sick, too?"

I didn't know. If the Angel did, he didn't have a word to say about it.

"Let's move," I said.

Before I could take another step, a single caw rang out in the branches above. I glanced up to meet the gaze of one crow—maybe the same one I'd seen here before, maybe not. The crow marked me with its gaze, then took wing, wheeling above us, its shadow running over the asphalt like black blood.

"That's not unsettling at all," Red said under his breath.

"Not even a little bit," I said.

I kept my senses peeled until we reached the spot that called to us, where the oaks on our left began to thin and the smog on the other side of the asphalt seemed to do the same. The last oak looked at us through a dozen whorled knots in its bark. Its leaves whispered and its branches swayed even though there was no breeze. Some of its roots floated above the soil, and some of them seemed to hold on to the earth around them for dear life.

Beth whistled. "How'd you get this thing to recognize you so fast? Usually, it takes more time to make that kind of friend."

I raised a brow.

"I mean, trees make the best portals between worlds," she said. "They're sentient. They know what they're doing when they open a door—or when they refuse to. Best if you can somehow key your-selves to the tree, or it to you. That way, there's no mistake. No one coming through who pretends to be you? Am I right?"

"No chameleons," I said.

"Exactly."

"I haven't done anything special to make friends," I said.

"Maybe it's the Angel," she said.

If the Angel had done something specific, I figured I would know. But the oak door recognizing the Angel? Entirely plausible.

"Whatever—however—I'll take it for now." I stepped aside, making way for Red to walk through the door first.

His hand brushed mine as he passed. Beth took Charlie's hand, and they walked through together.

I gave the In-Between one last long look before I entered the door-way. Nothing but sulfur and magical smog, asphalt and oaks. If the crow had taken up residence in the branches above me, I couldn't see it or hear it.

The In-Between looked and felt deserted, as if whatever had been living in it—or whatever spirit imbued it with sentience and presence —had left.

The thought made my skin crawl.

I backed into the oak. As soon as I passed completely into its space, its bark began to knit together again in front of me, replacing the yellow cast of the In-Between with tannin-soaked darkness, pushing my body backwards, squeezing the breath out of me until I popped into the human world again, the door closing fast behind me.

My boots thudded on familiar worn, white kitchen tile. My home away from home. Addie's house.

I checked the back door and windows—Addie had magicked new protections in the couple of hours since I'd called. They looked exactly like her halo—like the Milky Way, like the darkest night, and full of stars.

I inhaled the heavenly scent of coffee and frying bacon. The only light came from the bulb under the hood of the stove. The scarred oak table and chairs on the far side of the room were empty, the blinds in the windows behind them drawn, the winter chill and early morning hush before the dawn seeping in through the cracks and around the edges.

The spirit that kept and guarded Addie's house enveloped me, pressing on my skin, checking my identity and acknowledging me as welcome. Then it went on its way, ever vigilant.

Even with everything we'd been through, that welcome still felt somewhat miraculous. Addie and I didn't like each other all that much, but we needed each other. She was a Watcher—a descendant of the fallen angels known as the Nephilim—and she kept a weather eye on magical beings who entered her city, especially those uninvited. Like Rude, she was the magical law.

There was only one other person in her kitchen. Sunday Sloan.

Her rose-gold halo shone more red than gold, and she rested her hands on her hips the way she did when she was pissed but hadn't yet decided whom to take it out on. Her riot of blond curls hung to her shoulders. Shadows smudged the delicate skin underneath her dark blue eyes. She looked as pale as a ghost in her long black T-shirt and black pajama pants.

She looked behind me expectantly. Looking for the others.

Time spent between the worlds could be a funny thing, and I'd taken an extra minute or two in the In-Between, but I'd still expected to see everyone when I arrived. I didn't hear them either—no footsteps in the hall or on the stairs.

"Our people stepped through the door before I did. They should've arrived before me."

She narrowed her eyes.

If Red and the others weren't here, they'd somehow become lost between worlds—or lured off the path. Or they'd been taken. If Pestilence had—

Sunday's words echoed my next thought.

"Open another door, Night." She spun on her heel, flipping the switch on the burner under the bacon to OFF. She rushed toward the far counter, rummaging through the knife drawer and plucking a long, sharp blade from Addie's collection.

My magic still filled me, hovering at the edges of my skin. I let it run through my fingers and drew the sigil that Beth had shown me before. Then I let the magic fill my voice, and spoke the word of opening.

CHAPTER 5

THE AIR WHERE I'D traced the sigil began to glow, gilding the edges of the oak table and the steel appliances with light. Beside me, Sunday coiled, ready to leap through the door once it opened, her dark blue eyes fierce and her mouth set hard. She gripped the knife tightly.

My magic overflowed like floodwaters, breaching the dam of my skin. Anyone who challenged me would get the full-force brunt of it. Taken down. Destroyed.

Our people were in danger. We would find them and bring them home.

I took Sunday's free hand in mine. Any second now, the door would open.

The glow brightened. The stink of sulfur slid into the room.

The door into the In-Between cracked wide. I stepped forward.

Before I moved another inch, Red rushed through to our side, coughing. I backpedaled to make room just as Charlie and Beth staggered in behind him.

I spoke the word to close the door as soon as Beth cleared the glow. The door winked out as if it had never been there at all.

I tugged at the heart link with Red and felt him tug back. I wanted to trust that small proof that he was who he pretended to be, but I didn't know what had happened. I couldn't let that be enough. My magic was ready and waiting. I used it to slide into his mind, rifling through his memories until I came to one that no chameleon or other being could possibly have known about—the one I'd never shared with anyone but Red.

The night my parents died, after he'd found me in the backyard of my burning house and led me to safety. We'd spent the night in his closet, hidden from the cops and firefighters and the second round of Order assassins that came to clean up after the first.

If they'd found me, they'd have killed me. I was their target, after all, my parents just collateral damage.

Red hid me, bringing me food and water. I'd held on to his blond Lab, Dorothy, as if she were the only solid, safe thing in the whole world.

Now, I withdrew my magic from him and let him get a closer look at Charlie and Beth. His way was less intrusive. And it left me able to strike if I needed to.

Sunday stood at the ready, too, knife still in hand until everyone checked out. She tossed the blade back in its drawer. I let my magic ebb.

When it was all said and done, Charlie stood a foot from Sunday. I was behind him, so I couldn't see his face. The greenish cast of his halo had faded to the barest tint, allowing its natural color to shine through—literally. His halo shone like the sun on a cloudy day, a little wan, but clearly life-giving and life-preserving, a light in the dark and warmth against the cold. In its fully empowered state, without the sickness, I'd bet looking at him would be a little blinding.

Sunday stared at him, taking in every detail. She held herself completely still, as if moving or speaking would change something vital, or maybe make Charlie disappear.

He handled the words for her. "Wow," he said.

She swallowed hard. "Wow, what?"

"You're a lady."

Because she'd been older than him, but still a kid when they'd met. She'd been grown for a long time, but he was a teenager.

Sunday cracked a smile. "I wouldn't say that."

"What would you say?" he asked.

"I'm me," she said.

"But that doesn't mean anything."

"Are you really going to stand there and argue with me about it?" she asked.

He relaxed, his shoulders falling a good inch from where he'd held them high and tight.

I half-expected her to open her arms and hug him, even though Sunday didn't really do that sort of thing. What did you do when a person from your childhood showed up in your kitchen like this?

She reached out a hand.

Charlie didn't hesitate to take it. He gripped it firmly and shook. That seemed to satisfy them both.

Red laid a hand between my shoulder blades.

I met his gaze. "What happened?"

"No idea," he said. "We walked through the door, no problem. Then we just seemed to hang up. Like time stopped, and we stopped with it."

"Probably my fault," Charlie said. "Malek and Stacy did their best healing, but I'm still sick. Maybe it affects my magic."

That made sense, but only up to a point. "I thought you had to be knocked out to time travel."

"Not anymore," he said. "I grew into my power. I'm better at traveling than I used to be, aren't I? I can aim for where I want to go instead of ending up somewhere randomly. My evolution is messy. Things go crazy. Don't work the same way they always have. Then, all of a sudden they work better. This could be another evolution."

"But you don't know?" I asked.

He shrugged.

"You're making me nervous, Charlie Nobody," I said.

He squinted at me as if he were staring into a glare. "No one likes progress."

I snorted. "No one likes unpredictable effects on time and space. Puts a monkey in the wrench."

He squinted harder.

"What?" I asked.

"You look funny," he said.

Sunday glanced from Charlie to me and back again. "Funny how?"

"As if it's not just you standing there. As if there are two of you." He mulled that over. "I don't know what's happening to you," he said. "But it's making me nervous, Night."

He wasn't the only one. And he didn't know me, which probably made the feeling worse. "Fair enough."

I looked at Red again. "You feel anyone's hand on that 'hang up' other than Charlie's here?"

Red shook his head. A thick lock of salt-and-pepper hair fell into his eyes. He pushed it back with both hands. "I didn't feel anything at all, Night. Not the air on my skin or the breath in my lungs. I just froze there, the wheels in my mind turning and panic firing up a half second later once I realized what'd happened."

"Smell? Taste?" I asked.

He shook his head.

"See anything?"

"No," he said.

"Sensory deprivation."

He nodded.

I didn't like the sound of that, and I seriously didn't like not knowing what had caused it.

Beth had been conspicuously silent. Maybe she knew something we didn't. "What about you?"

"Sorry," she said. "If it helps, I tried to reach out to Malek through the magical connection we have. I couldn't feel him either."

This was sounding worse by the second. "So, Charlie—you're right, and your magic is changing. Or there's a glitch with the In Between. Or magical doorways aren't working the way they should. Or—"

Red finished my sentence. "Someone's messing with us."

"Or it could be something we haven't thought of yet," Sunday said.

I nodded. "We need to take a closer look. Start eliminating options. Narrow it down. Talk to Addie."

I glanced toward the door as the Watcher in question cleared her throat from her newfound perch, leaning against the doorjamb. The stars in her halo burned brightly.

She wore her hair as she always did, pulled into a bun at the crown of her head. The sulfur in the room had dissipated enough that I could smell the sweet coconut scent of the moisturizer she'd applied to her dark brown skin and, woven with it, a touch of amber perfume. She'd pushed the sleeves of her gold tunic toward her elbows and rolled the hems of her black jeans above the heels of her bare feet.

The brown eyes behind her silver-framed glasses traveled the room, her gaze resting on each of us in turn and lingering on Charlie.

"You the time traveler?" she asked.

"Yes, ma'am," he said.

"Addie. Or Ms. Johnson. Are you feeling all right?"

He nodded.

"Good," she said. "Because we have a situation in the basement."

"We just had a situation," Beth said.

Addie pursed her lips. "How is this different from any other day lately?"

Beth touched a finger to her temple. "Point."

I met Addie's gaze. "What's in the basement?"

"Not a what," she said. "A girl who had a close encounter with an archangel."

I'd been visited by an archangel before, in person and in my dreams—Michael, the one whom I descended from, whose blood ran in my veins and enabled me to host *La Muerte* without disintegrating. So far, Michael had shown up only to ask for my help. When I'd needed his desperately, he'd arrived on the scene too little, too late.

Beth and Kevin had told us that Gabriel was in Portland. That they had confirmed magical knowledge of it.

"You're holding a girl prisoner in the basement," I said.

Addie shook her head. "She wanted to stay down there. Said it would shield her presence from prying eyes. She won't talk to me much. She wants to talk to you, Night."

I pushed my way past Beth and Addie, into the hall. I caught a glimpse of the living room to my left—the reflection of the Christmas tree's glow on the hardwood floor, the empty, crouching forms of the sofas, the strong protections on the front door and windows. Then I turned my back on those things, turning right toward the basement door.

Addie jogged to catch up, and the others followed.

"What did Gabriel do to her?" I asked.

"He woke her magic."

Given what we'd learned in Houston, that fit his M.O. So, this girl was the one. Important enough for an archangel to hunt her down and gift her with magic out of nowhere. What was she? What was she meant for?

It seemed too easy to assume that she was Pestilence's vessel. There were plenty of other magicians in the city for the Horseman to choose. But what if she was the one he sought? What then?

"Who's watching the girl?" I asked.

"The house spirit."

If it was just a girl—albeit a girl with magic—the house spirit could certainly handle that. I'd feel better if the two kids who should be here were watching her, though. Ben, the shield. Jess, the Watcher-in-training.

The thought flashed across my face. Addie answered the obvious question. "Ben and Jess are at Corey's house."

Red sounded off behind us. "Talking to her folks?"

"Bingo," Addie said. "As of last night."

What Red had intended to do.

"Any idea how that's going?" he asked.

"None. But I haven't received any emergency texts yet, so I'm taking that as a good sign."

If Ben and Jess were dealing with Corey's parents, then Red didn't need to go there unless the kids needed backup. Just as well—we needed him here.

"They'll be back soon?" I asked.

"When they're ready."

They could take care of themselves. And, at any rate, there was no stopping them once they decided to do something. They were powers in their own right. We'd all learned the futility of trying to boss them.

I reached for the basement door. For a second, the knob refused to turn under my hand—the house spirit, doing its job. One breath later, it granted me access.

The single bulb above the landing glared, its tarnished pull chain glinting in the light. I descended the stairs two at a time, hitting the bottom landing with both feet. A left turn took me through the basement's locked-down layer of magical protection—like walking through a magical waterfall—into the basement proper.

My gaze slid to the side door first, confirming that it remained protected just like the rest of the entrances to the house. It was colder down here, the chill creeping in through the concrete walls and floor, which Addie had made less painful to sit on by laying down an assortment of rugs and pillows. Our girl sat on the ocean-blue rug and pillow furthest from the stairs.

She had a strip of black hair down the middle, long enough to be gelled into a powerful Mohawk, but she hadn't bothered. The ends were wet from the ubiquitous cold drizzle of the season.

Her halo looked like a dark mirror. A psychic's halo, bright and raw and brand new. She would be gifted visions every so often. Maybe she'd have control over them, maybe not.

She smelled of fear—she was scared of what had happened to her, of what it meant, and of every single one of us here.

She looked at me with eyes the color of a rain-drenched green field. Freckles dotted her cheeks and nose, her light brown complexion waxen. Black leather earrings cut into the shape of feathers brushed the tops of her shoulders. She wore a dark gray hoodie, holey, faded jeans, and gray wool socks. She looked to be in her mid-twenties.

I glanced behind me as Addie stepped through the protections, and Red after her. He eyed the girl closely, reading her soul. After a moment, he met my gaze and nodded. She was exactly what she appeared to be.

It was Charlie who startled me by finally making his way downstairs and through the protections in that moment. His eyes widened at the sight of the girl.

"You," he said. "Luna."

She turned her gaze to him. Her jaw dropped. "Charlie?"

"How is it you?" he asked. "I can't believe it."

I looked from him to her and back again. "What's going on here?"

"I know her," he said. "I met her…" He counted on his fingers.

She filled in the blanks. "Five years ago. But you don't look a day older than you did then. How do you explain that? Is that magic, too?"

He looked at me. "I was on the run from the Horseman—before he made me sick. He chased me across time, onto a cold, dead-end street. But it wasn't here. Where was it?"

Her voice filled with wonder. "Denver."

"Right. Denver. Anyway, I didn't have a coat, or a pair of shoes for that matter, and snow was coming down so thick I couldn't see my own hand in front of my face. I had nothing left, magically. I was all tapped out. She took me in for the night. Gave me half of her hamburger and fries. Kept me safe."

So, Luna was a good person. She probably saved Charlie's life. "What are the odds she's the one Gabriel dosed? That she ended up here, where you are?"

"It can't be a coincidence," he said.

I shook my head. "No such thing."

"She was meant to come here," Charlie said. "We're meant to help her."

Luna's voice sounded older than she looked, roughened by cigarette smoke. "That's why I'm here. That's why my vision led me here. Addie said to wait for the woman named Night. You're the one I'm waiting for?"

I nodded.

"You know my name," she said. "If Charlie is your friend, then I trust I'm safe here."

"You had a vision?" I asked.

"After—the thing that changed me—I saw Addie's face and the address. That's all there is to it." After a moment, she added, "I can tell you're measuring what kind of threat I am. It's in your eyes."

"Are you a threat?" I asked.

"I'm exhausted. I'm freaked out. And I've stepped into something bad and big. Or it stepped on me." She shook her head. "I understand threats. How they hold themselves. How they talk. I've lived with them most of my life. You're the biggest threat in this room."

She wasn't wrong.

"You understand what happened to you?" I asked.

She glanced over my shoulder, nodding at the crowd that had followed me down. "Addie explained. I still don't believe it. Not really. But what else am I supposed to do? Pretending it's not happening— pretending all of you people are crazy—that won't wash, either."

Her halo hadn't shifted when she spoke. She was steady on the inside. Her new, raw magic was steady, too. I saw no sign of a lie in her.

I looked to Addie from the corner of my eye. She shrugged as if to say, *what you see is what you get.*

I made my way into the circle of rugs and pillows, lowering myself to sit across from her. "The archangel? When did he show up?"

She chewed her lip. "While I was walking home from my bar shift. I was headed down Naito, just under the Broadway Bridge, and they— they just, *poof.* You know, appeared? Scared the shit out of me. They shone. Like the halo around the sun during an eclipse. Like they were made of darkness *and* light. Their eyes were made of light, too. Faded jeans. White sweater—what do you call them?—fisherman's sweater. Brown leather boots. Golden hair, sticking up everywhere. Androgynous. And when they talked? Damn. Like big church bells. Deafening."

I took in her description and matched it with my own experience with Michael. Not the same, but definitely in the same ballpark. "What did he say?"

"They, not he."

"Because…"

"They're somewhere between male and female."

"Okay," I said. "What did they say?"

"My name." She rubbed her palms on her thighs. "The sound almost knocked me over. Like, my legs didn't want to hold me up. And then they said I would be needed. Pressure started to build in my head and my heart was pounding and I thought I was maybe having a stroke? And then I dropped like a rock right there on the sidewalk. When I came to, they were gone. I was only out a few minutes. But the world looked completely different. All the familiar things—the cars parked on the sides of the road and the arcs of the bridge and the empty sound of the night, they all seemed like strangers. Then the vision came."

Her world would never look the same again. It would never feel the same again, either. I hated to ask my next question, but it had to be done. "I need to take a look at your memory and make sure there's nothing you missed."

She cocked her head.

"Your conscious mind knows what you saw and you're telling me everything you remember," I said.

"Yeah."

"But your subconscious might have picked up something important."

She mulled that over. "How would you do this? In theory, that is."

"With my magic," I said.

She curled her hands into fists. "Will it hurt?"

"No," I said. "It might feel a little uncomfortable. Most people aren't used to having an extra person in their mind. You should know that you won't be able to hide anything from me. And that, if I think you are, and I think the secret is relevant to what we're dealing with, I'll pursue it—whether you want me to or not."

Her eyes widened. A stream of questions flashed across them: Why should she trust me? Would I use what I found against her? What gave me the right to threaten to violate her mind?

When she opened her mouth again, she asked a different question. "What are you dealing with?"

"The end of the world," I said.

"Seriously?"

"Unfortunately."

Red backed me up. "I know it sounds unhinged, but it's real."

After a moment, she said, "I saw an archangel with my own two eyes. They did something to me. You don't sound as crazytown to me as you would have yesterday. Really."

Charlie made his way over to sit beside her. She flashed him a forced grin.

"It's okay," he said.

After a moment, she nodded.

I slid a thread of magic into her mind, past meager normal defenses. I felt her fear as if it were my own, visceral and barely contained on a leash of bravado. I saw us as she did, through her eyes —strangers, like the rest of the world had become, bristling with a power she could sense but didn't understand. Her moments with Gabriel pooled on the surface of her other memories like an offering.

Gabriel appeared just as she'd said. I could make out a little more of their appearance—wings that had no color of their own, but weren't translucent either. They picked up the colors of their environment, the way certain lizards did, their skin turning the color of bark or a blade of grass. The archangel stepped toward her, leaving a trail of smoking, glowing footprints on the rain-slick sidewalk.

Gabriel spoke to her. Their voice echoed inside her head only, not on the street. The words were for her alone. The memory matched what she'd told me—except for one thing. After her legs had given way and she'd tumbled to the concrete, the cars and the bridge and the night turning gray and fuzzy, Gabriel had drawn closer, kneeling beside her to whisper in her ear.

I'm sorry that you're not ready for this, the archangel said. *I pray it works out for you.*

Then the world, and Gabriel with it, went entirely dark, and Luna ceased to hear or see another thing.

I slipped out of her mind and back into my own, blinking with the transition. She looked at me with something like wonder.

"I was there with you," she said softly. "How did you do that?"

"It's who I am," I said.

Fear filled her words. "What did they mean by, 'I pray it works out for you'?"

Before I could answer, something shifted in the dark mirror of her halo—it began to melt like film melted under too much heat.

The Angel of Death's wings fluttered inside my rib cage.

Luna's eyes emptied, then filled again with awareness. Her jaw dropped. "What are you, Night? My eyes—I see you, and I see something dark, like a shadow behind you. It has wings. Is it another angel?"

The melted places in her halo began to glow like coals in a dying fire.

I rolled to my feet and launched myself toward her. She tried to push away from me, digging in with her heels, but her socks slipped on the weave of the rug. She couldn't get any traction.

I took her face in my hands, her skin radiating too much heat. "Luna, something's wrong."

"You," she said. "You're wrong."

I shot a look over my shoulder to Beth, who was already running towards us. "Her magic—it's burning."

Luna sucked in a breath and held it. Her muscles went rigid.

Charlie and Beth helped me lay Luna flat. Beth touched her wrist to Luna's forehead, wincing as she drew it back. She laid a finger on one of the glyphs tattooed on her forearm—brand new ink, created in the last couple of days, but already healed.

I knew instinctively that healing was what the glyph did. Or it was supposed to. Its magic did nothing for Luna's burning halo, her burning magic. The girl was going up from the inside out.

Beth fumbled for the knife she carried. To cut herself and release the poison blood in her veins. She'd been able to turn back death with it once before. Maybe she could do it again.

But the Angel knew differently—it wouldn't be fast enough. It wouldn't *be* enough.

I closed my eyes, feeling for the Angel's presence inside, drawing on my magic and his. I didn't know what we could do. I didn't know how to tap the Angel's power—or whether it could overtake what was happening to Luna. I only knew we had to do something.

My magic lived in my heart. Hers might, too.

A beat before my fingertips brushed the fabric over Luna's chest, she turned to ash. Not just her halo, but all of her. She froze just like that, holding her human form, but still and broken into thousands of gray shards held together by a whisper.

I screamed her name.

The wind from my lungs was enough to break her.

She exploded into a cascade of ashes, rising in the air and fluttering back to ground like ghastly flower petals.

Beth stared, shaking, at what remained of Luna. Her mouth worked, but no words came.

Charlie held on to Beth, fingernails digging into her arms. Beth pulled away before he could draw blood—and poison along with it.

I rolled back on my heels, overbalancing, and sat down hard. Shadows danced on the floor around us, cast by the living as they drew close to the dead.

I glanced up to see Red beside me.

He hunkered down, one hand on my shoulder. He rubbed his mouth with the other. "Jesus, Night."

That didn't sound like blame. It didn't feel like it, either. Still, if I'd known what to do—if I'd done it in time, I could've helped her. I didn't know how, but there had to be a way. There had to have been something.

The Angel of Death should've helped. He had power over death. He hadn't lifted a finger. He hadn't said a word to me.

Why?

At this point, I couldn't think of a single reason he would withhold information or aid. That left the only reason he hadn't stepped up.

He couldn't have done anything to save Luna.

"I saw what happened," Red said. "The magic Gabriel woke in her —she couldn't handle it. She couldn't hold it. It was working on her before she even got here, breaking down her body, breaking down her soul."

I met his gaze. "Her soul."

He nodded. "It's gone."

"Not gone on?"

"Nothing left," he said. "She's destroyed."

Why would an archangel do something like that to Luna? To some unsuspecting girl? It'd never occurred to me that their magical gift could have these kinds of consequences. Why give magic to a girl whose molecular structure couldn't contain it? Why give magic when it had a chance of destroying the recipient?

This was war. That was why.

The magic they'd given to Luna was needed. Need mattered more than anything—sure as hell it mattered more than consideration for Luna.

If the magic killed Luna, would Gabriel try to gift it to someone else? Would they be able to handle it? What if they couldn't? Would they die as well? Would this pattern repeat itself until Gabriel found a stable candidate?

All those questions boiled down to one for me: What was I going to do about it?

And on the heels of that, the realization of what had just happened. Luna, dead.

She wasn't an enemy. She wasn't one of my many victims. She was a girl who'd come to us—to me—for help. I'd failed her.

Red's gentle drawl broke into my thoughts. "Wait a second, Night."

I looked at him.

"I can see what you're feeling. Hell, I can feel it. You can't go chasing after Gabriel. Not with a Horseman in town."

Sunday offered me a hand up. "Keep your eye on the prize, Night."

I glanced at her.

"Don't give me that look," she said.

Charlie let go of Beth, finally. He stood up slowly, bent over, resting his hands on his thighs. "What look?"

"The one that says fuck me, she'll do what she wants."

I took her hand and let her pull me to my feet. "We need a handle on it all. I can't have this happening to people—people who never asked for it, who have no idea what Gabriel's done to them. Either their lives are irrevocably changed when the magic comes alive inside them, or they're like Luna. One second here, and gone the next. It's not right."

"Add it to the list," Sunday said. "Anyway, how is this any different than our experience, our magic?"

"You're kidding, right?"

She shook her head.

"We were born with magic," I said.

"That manifested in us at some point when we were young. Could've been when we were two or three, or when we hit puberty, or somewhere in between. All of it unexpected. All of it life-changing. What's being disowned and abandoned? How is it different than being dead?"

To a lot of kids, it wasn't different at all. It colored my tone, even if my words were meant for Sunday in particular. "You're still here. You're grown and you make your own rules."

Comparison was a smokescreen. None of the threats we'd faced compared to any of the others. I trained my gaze on Addie, who'd been conspicuously silent.

"Is Gabriel still in town?" I asked.

She stared back at me, her expression unreadable. "No."

That was something. I held on to it. "Is Luna the only one he made?"

"Yes," she said.

"You're sure?"

"I'd stake my life on it," she said.

Charlie cleared his throat. "Is Pestilence here?"

Addie met his gaze. "I felt a presence enter the city while we were talking with Luna, one of the most powerful presences I've ever felt. I couldn't identify it precisely because it's not embodied. I'm going to say yes."

"Is Pestilence still here?" I asked. "Or did he pass through?"

She looked at her feet for a moment, her glasses slipping a bit on her nose. She used her index finger to push them back into place. "Still here."

What now?

A voice near my heart spoke so softly, I barely heard it.

Luna knows.

Two words that exploded inside of me.

I spoke to the Angel. *Did you say that?*

His voice reverberated. *Not me.*

Then who?

He didn't answer—perhaps because he didn't know.

I'd start to wonder whether I'd imagined the voice. Or whether I'd misunderstood and the voice had only been my own. But it didn't feel like either of those things. It felt real. So real I couldn't ignore it.

I glanced around the room. All eyes had turned to me.

"It's possible that he's after someone else in the city. That his and Gabriel's paths intersecting in Portland is a coincidence," I said.

Sunday shook her head. "Like you said, you don't believe in those, and neither do the rest of us."

"I can't shake the feeling that Luna is important," I said.

"She's dead and gone," Sunday said. "It doesn't matter anymore."

"But it does," I said.

"How do you know?"

I tried to figure out how to explain. "It's a gut feeling."

That wasn't quite right, but it did the job. No Order operative ignored those kinds of feelings. Refusing to listen to a gut feeling—animal instinct—got people killed.

"Okay," Sunday said. "What do you want to do?"

"I don't know." My senses felt used up, my head filled with cobwebs. "I need to get quiet. Listen."

"You need to sleep, Night," Addie said. "You need food. You're running on empty."

Addie was right, but there was something I needed to do first, and need mattered more than anything.

"Let me—" I literally couldn't say the words *clean up Luna's ashes.* I started again. "Luna should have a proper burial."

Charlie straightened. "I'll help."

I shook my head. "I want to do it."

"She was my friend, Night."

I wanted to deny him. I wanted to do this by myself. I didn't want to have to make small talk or listen too closely to any other kind of talk. I needed to release grief. Shock. I needed to let my breathing expand so that I could think—or at least open the door to eventual thoughts.

"Okay," I said. "Charlie and me."

Red laid a hand on my shoulder and squeezed. I reached up to brush my fingers across his.

He led the others out. Charlie and I watched them go, one by one slipping through the protections and vanishing from our sight. Addie stayed until the last of them had gone.

"Thank you, both of you," she said

Then she turned and walked away. I couldn't hear her climb the stairs or shut the basement door behind her, but I felt her all the same. She might've kept her face composed and a tight rein on her feelings, but I'd seen her halo and the way the swirling stars inside it dimmed.

It spoke volumes.

Grief that Luna had come to her for help and died before she could receive it. Fear that, even if we'd had more time, we couldn't have done a thing for the girl. And a deeper fear, one heavy enough that it seemed to make the air tremble.

What if we couldn't handle what was coming? What if we were only pretending we had a chance in hell?

I knew exactly how she felt. My heart hurt.

I took a deep breath and blew it out slowly. I brushed as many of Luna's ashes from my clothes as I could—by no means all of them.

I'd seen a lot of dead people in my life, and I'd killed most of those. I'd never seen anything like what had happened to Luna.

Sunday's question spun in my mind: What did I want to do? And on the heels of that, another bloomed like a poisonous flower.

Whose voice had echoed inside my heart?

CHAPTER 6

I PUT ONE FOOT in front of the other on my way to the room Red and I shared, ducking inside and snicking the door shut behind me. The space was close enough to the kitchen to smell like bacon. In front of me, the bathroom was dark except for a night-light that glowed on the far wall. To my right, the bed beckoned, as did the man who'd already shrugged out of his clothes and climbed in.

The green and brown light of his halo, along with sacred heart tattoo on his chest, shone with subdued light—his magic remained powerful, but he was bone tired.

I studied him, thinking about what Beth had said. His magic looked no different to me than before, but she hadn't said his magic had changed, had she? She'd only talked about what his magic meant.

He trained his sleepy green eyes on mine. "Everything go all right?"

I sighed, loosening the rest of the tension that remained in my muscle and bone. My shoulders dropped a solid inch. "Charlie cried. Silent tears."

"You?"

I slipped off my shoes and socks—which I'd have done as soon as I entered the house if I'd come through the front door like a normal person instead of appearing in the kitchen through a magical doorway.

"No."

"You angry?" he asked.

I shrugged, plenty of impatience soaked into the gesture. "Sad and angry and frustrated. And someone's talking to me."

His expression grew serious. "Angel?"

I shook my head, kicking off my jeans on the way to bed and tossing them, along with my shirt, onto the closest chair. I felt a chill in the air that the heat hadn't chased away—or maybe the chill came from inside. Goosebumps rose along my skin.

Red folded back the covers, inviting me underneath. I climbed in, sliding towards his warmth.

"Who, then?" he asked.

"Mystery voice," I said.

"What'd it say?"

"Luna knows."

He furrowed his brow. "Jesus, Night."

"I know. It felt natural, as if it was a part of me—but not."

"You've already got two people in there," he said. "That seems like plenty."

"I agree." I combed my fingers through my hair.

"You're worried."

"Yes," I said.

He considered what I'd said, then sighed. "Feels like we're underwater."

"In over our heads?"

He nodded.

"There's no way to know for sure," I said. No blueprint. No footsteps to follow. The worlds had been in plenty of danger before—deadly danger, more than once—but never like this.

He rolled onto his side to face me. "I trust you, Night."

"I trust you, too." With everything—my heart, my life, my family.

"I'm not talking about that," he said. "I'm talking about the other thing. The wings. Whatever comes along with that."

The Angel. "Before we invaded the Order, Beth told me that there was a chance I might not just be the Angel's vessel, but that I might actually become the Angel of Death. That seemed impossible until—"

He finished my thought. "The wings."

I closed my eyes for a moment, gathering the right words. When I looked out again, I gazed into Red's eyes and breathed in the solid, strong grass and earth of his magic. I felt the pull of the heart link between us.

"I finally figured out how not to be a monster. How to be human."

"You weren't a monster."

"Oh? I didn't use my magic to kill people? I didn't do that for years, no questions asked, completely and utterly sure that every single person whose mind I took and whose fears I turned against them deserved what they got?"

He sighed. "You didn't kill Faith."

No, I hadn't. Did that one redeeming factor outweigh all the terrible things I'd done?

The Order had sent me on a mission to kill a child. I'd had no problem murdering her parents, but when I'd gotten to Faith, I hadn't been able to pull the magical trigger. I'd seen my own terrible childhood in her—parents who didn't understand my power and thought it was rooted in evil, the abuse they'd perpetrated when they'd tried to help me, and no future, because what kind of future could there possibly be when today was misery. I'd looked at her and known right away that I could never raise a hand against her personally.

But if I didn't kill her, the Order would send someone else to complete my mission. That left only one choice if I wanted to save her. I'd taken her with me and fled the Order—the only family I'd known for most of my life and the only home I remembered—forever. We'd lived on the run, under threat of death.

All the killing I'd done had an unanticipated effect on me—it had literally destroyed my soul. By the time I'd made the split-second decision to take Faith and run, there'd been nothing left of me on the inside.

Until the souls of the people I'd killed had followed me, haunting me, forged themselves into one and took the place of my ruined soul —a gift that I didn't deserve, and one I tried to be worthy of.

"The choices I've made since that night have been good ones," I said. "I've helped people. That counts for something."

"It counts for everything," he said.

I shook my head. "I may never be able to wash away all the blood on my hands."

"You never stop trying, Night."

No, I didn't. The people I'd killed might have cobbled together a new soul for me—a second chance to get it right. But it was up to me to take that chance and run with it as far and as fast and as well as I could. I didn't consider my soul to be complete. It was my job to continue to forge it every single day.

"I'm doing my best," I said. "I hope it's good enough."

Red took that in. "No one can say you've done wrong—taking the Angel into yourself, fighting Shadow, bringing down your mentor and saving those kids, dropping the End on his ass. You had to do all those things. There wasn't anyone else who could do what you did. More important than that, it's who you are."

He understood. He really did. "Thank you for saying that."

"You don't have to thank me. I see you."

That was his magic as I understood it. Beth believed him to be something far more powerful. I couldn't speak to that, only to what he meant to me. Who he was.

"I love you," I said.

"I love you, too, babe."

I searched his eyes for a hint of unease, a hint of fear about what might be coming. It was there. He was worried.

"What if Beth is right about me?" I asked.

"What if you become the Angel of Death?"

I nodded. "She talks to me as if it's a foregone conclusion."

He looked into me, his magic flowing strong and steady. I held my breath.

After a moment, he said, "I don't see any changes in your soul."

I sighed in relief. "Nothing?"

"Not a single thing." He reached out a hand to brush a wayward strand of hair from my face. "You're still you."

"For now." There was no way to know how long that would remain true.

"Always," he said. "I'm not leaving."

It struck me hard, the wonder in that. "You don't know what you're signing up for."

"No one ever does."

I turned my head to kiss his palm. When I looked at him again, I read desire in his eyes—he wanted me, Night, and nothing else mattered. In that moment, the world and all of its terrible possibilities fell away.

He held my gaze, drawing me closer until I could feel the electric edge of his halo. He brushed his lips across mine, then deepened the kiss. I reveled in the taste of him, the gentle-rough insistence of his hands as they roamed my curves.

The heart link between us flared. I felt his love and his need. They mirrored my own.

He hooked his thumbs beneath the sides of my panties and drew them down, then moved close enough to mold the front of his body to mine. I wrapped my leg around his waist. He slid into me, never tearing away his gaze, never closing his eyes.

We lay joined for a moment, so close and so connected that I could feel his heartbeat, and he felt mine. Then we began to move, love and lust, instinct and pleasure taking the reins, driving us into each other, two made one.

Afterwards, I tucked my head beneath his chin and listened to his racing heart calm. My breathing deepened. My eyes wanted to close.

"Turn over?" Red asked.

I nodded, rolling away from him, onto my side. He drew closer, molding his body to mine, draping his arm between my breasts and resting his palm over my heart. I felt safe and held for the space of a few precious minutes before sleep pulled me under.

The dream took me completely, swallowing me whole. There was no preamble, no attempt to lull me or ease me in.

I stood inside the branch of the Order we'd taken down, but not in the portion that existed within the human realm—in the adjacent angelic realm. The place where, once up on a time, the Order had imprisoned the Angel of Death. The place that they'd turned into a feeding ground for the End, where they'd given him the magical children who hadn't made the grade as assassin or chameleon material.

My feet rested on the granite stair landing in front of the destroyed platform beneath the Order compound where the Angel and I, using the combined magic of my adopted family, had killed my mentor and banished the End. The crude stone cage on the platform that had once been a door to the End's realm of ice stood truly empty. It contained nothing, and it went nowhere.

The light here had dimmed to the softest glow. There were no chameleons to guard the place, because there was nothing and no one to guard. I could hear the rush of blood in my own veins and mark the beating of my heart in the hush. The air felt unnaturally warm against my skin.

I turned to scan the giant staircase behind me, but saw no one. I listened with all of my being, but heard no one. Until the sudden rush of flames erupting on the platform focused my attention.

Michael.

He materialized beside the empty cage, stepping off the platform and walking toward me, his every step shaking the stone underfoot. His hair was made of fire, writhing flames of orange, yellow, red, and blue. He had three eyes, two in the usual places and a third in the center of his forehead. He wore golden armor that glittered like diamonds, and a sword with a golden hilt sheathed on his back.

The right hand of God. The fiery sword of protection. My ancestor.

Just as before, the glamour he wore faded. He became a regular-looking guy—one who threw off enough power to bend the air around his body—and, given how close he stood to me now, the air around my body as well. He wore a pair of faded jeans and a black T-shirt that looked as if it'd been washed a hundred times, embossed with once-white script that read *Ride the Lightning*. He had black hair, short and thick, and eyes the color of the sun.

His voice sounded like thunder to my ears, and like a tenor's whisper inside my head.

"Thanks for coming," he said.

I couldn't help it—I burst out laughing. "This is your party. You brought me here. What about?"

"Gabriel," he said. "He never makes a mistake."

"Thanks for that confirmation," I said.

He frowned at my sarcasm. "Pestilence is circling closer."

"Tell me something I don't already know," I said.

Michael's frown deepened. He laid a hand over my heart, the seat of my magic. The magic that emanated from him seemed to slide through my skin—through my cells—straight into me. For a brief second, I thought I felt something inside of me come loose. Or unlock.

"Your soul is speaking to you," he said.

"The voice I heard before?"

He nodded. "You should listen."

I didn't understand. "Back up. How can my soul speak to me? It's part of me."

"No," he said. "It's not. And you're running out of time."

My soul wasn't part of me? What was that supposed to mean? I opened my mouth to ask, but different words rolled off my tongue.

"Time's the enemy," I said. "I won't have enough time to find the vessel before Pestilence does."

"You have more time than most. Maybe you'll succeed after all." Michael narrowed his eyes. His voice dropped an octave. "Be careful, Night."

"As careful as I can be," I said.

He shook his head. "You were a monster. Now, you're human—or mostly so. Be careful you don't become that which you hate and fear."

He drew his hand away and, with it, the dream.

My eyes opened in a flash. I lay flat on my back, gaze directed toward the ceiling. A big black spider clung to the white paint, all of its many eyes locked on me. After a moment, it skittered away to hunt smaller prey.

A cold sweat sheened my forehead and at the nape of my neck, my breath skimming the surface of my lungs, my heart pounding. Red slept beside me, the sound of his gentle snoring reminding me that I was solid flesh and blood and bones, helping me to settle back into my body.

Michael hadn't done much to change my opinion of him—once an asshole, always an asshole. He never showed up when I needed him, only when he needed something from me. Or, in this case, when he wanted to dispense a mystery when I didn't need one more. And a warning—in this case, one that mirrored my own thoughts so closely, I didn't want to be reminded.

Thinking about what was happening to me and talking about it with Red were very different things than hearing the same words spout from the mouth of an archangel. I didn't like Michael, but he hadn't lied to me.

I slipped out of bed, careful not to wake Red. I ducked into the bathroom for a quick splash of water on my face, but it didn't do much to revive my pre-dream calm or my tired body. I dressed quickly and quietly, making my way down the hall and into the kitchen.

A little further down the hall, the glow of the Christmas tree lights cheered the dark living room. The sofa that faced in my direction held a sleeping someone wrapped in a rumpled down comforter. The doors and windows were locked, the house spirit on guard.

Sunday sat at the far end of the scarred oak table, legs curled beneath her. Her rose-gold halo had settled down toward gold. She'd changed out of her pajamas into a pair of snug black pants and a black button-down shirt, open with a gray tank underneath. She'd tucked her blond curls behind her ears, and she still had a full set of luggage beneath her dark blue eyes.

She'd raised the blinds on the back windows and stared out into the rain-drenched backyard, lost in her thoughts—although, even in that state, she was aware of me. A half-full mug of coffee and a half dozen crisp slices of bacon on a grease-soaked paper towel rested in front of her.

She wasn't alone. Miguel sat at the foot of the table, staring into an extra tall mug of coffee, absent-mindedly running one hand over the tangled, wet mess of his short black hair. His purple bruise of a halo looked extra bruised today—he was worried. He shoved the sleeves of his black turtleneck to his elbows. The hems of his black jeans were wet from the rain. He wriggled his wool sock-clad toes and glanced up, brown eyes meeting mine.

He'd volunteered to take care of things at the gym for Red and me while we traveled to Texas—not his natural habitat, although he'd never had trouble staying fit enough, working inside the Order.

Miguel hadn't been an operative like Sunday and me; he'd been chosen to guard the Angel of Death during the time the Order had held him. The mentors had put Miguel through a program of torturous change, remaking his natural magic. He was a valuable ally as a chameleon, someone who could impersonate anyone down to the smallest physical detail, even down to their magic. He's stood by us when the going got deadly, which made him more than an ally. He was a friend. He was my brother.

"Everything go okay at the gym?" I asked.

"Like clockwork," he said. "Not so much here—Sunday filled me in."

"When it rains," I said, leaving him to fill in the second half of the sentence.

He narrowed his eyes. "You look a little off, Night. Something else happen?"

Having heard that, Sunday broke her trance and turned her gaze toward me. She frowned.

"That exact expression," I said. "That's how I feel. Any of those bacon slices for me?"

She handed me the whole plate. "What's up?"

"Michael," I said.

"That asshole."

I raised a slice to her and took a bite. I relayed the dream to her and Miguel. I left nothing out.

Sunday took a minute to mull over my words. "What's your soul saying?"

"Luna knows."

"I'll bite," Miguel said. "What does she know?"

"That's just it," I said.

Sunday sighed. "You don't know."

I shook my head.

"I don't like this, Night." She closed her eyes. When she looked out again, she looked a little more lost than she had when I'd first walked in. "What does having more time than most mean?"

"That, I have a clue about," I said. "We have a time traveler in the house."

Miguel took a swig of his coffee. "Charlie, asleep on the couch."

I nodded. "He's sick, and his magic is tweaking itself, so it's not one-hundred-percent predictable. But."

"It's a tool," Sunday said. "We should use it."

"Charlie's not a thing," Miguel said. "He might have different opinions about our using his magic, depending on what we want to do with it. I'm assuming that you have an idea, Night?"

"Yep. Go back and get Luna before Gabriel doses her."

Miguel pressed his lips into a thin line. "If you were Gabriel, would you be down with that?"

"Probably not," I said.

"So you're okay with earning us an archangel enemy?"

"I don't really care about Gabriel here—at least, not that way. Michael told me that Gabriel never makes mistakes."

Sunday shook her head. "So he killed Luna on purpose?"

"Or he dosed her with magic, which made her psychic and drew her to us," I said. "Either way, what he did ensured that Luna would die."

"That's fucked up, Night."

I grabbed her mug and downed the rest of her lukewarm coffee in one swallow, grimacing at the sweetness of the sugar she'd added. "It's for sure bullshit."

Miguel studied his hands, then looked at me. "We should talk to Charlie. Get his take."

Sunday set her feet on the floor and pushed away from the table, the chair legs scraping on the tile. "Let's wake him up."

We made our way into the front of the house. The Christmas tree lights turned the whole space into a kaleidoscope, from the long oak dining table on the right with its always-full bowl of fruit in the center to the dark fireplace on the left, the family photos on the mantle, and the two sofas positioned in front of the hearth with the coffee table crouching low between them.

Charlie had kicked off the down comforter, leaving it puddled near his bare feet. A film of sweat sheened his brow and wetted the ends of his hair. He'd shrugged out of his suspenders, which tangled around his waist.

Sunday perched on the edge of the coffee table. Miguel and I crowded behind her. She reached out to shake Charlie gently, but his eyes fluttered open before she touched him. Sleep clouded them for a moment before his gaze cleared. He took in the sight of us as if he'd expected to see us—including Miguel, whom he'd yet to meet.

"Hey," Charlie said to Miguel.

"You know who I am?" Miguel asked.

"The chameleon."

Miguel nodded.

Charlie cleared his throat. He didn't ask about Pestilence or Gabriel or Luna or anything I expected.

"You want to know about my magic," he said.

Sunday blinked at him. "How do you know that?"

"Michael told me," he said.

"You dreamed about him?" I asked.

Charlie nodded. "Just like you."

No way he could know that. Unless there was more to him than I'd guessed. Or unless the archangel had told him about our conversation.

"You want to try something, don't you, Night?" he asked.

Sunday looked at me. "She's always trying something."

"I was just thinking—when you travel through time, how much control do you have over what time you arrive?" I asked.

"How far back do you want to go?" he asked.

CHAPTER 7

THE WINTER CHILL that seeped through the basement's concrete floor and walls sent a shiver down my spine. The protections and the house spirit seemed to hem us in instead of keeping unwanted people and spirits out. It felt downright claustrophobic. The fine hairs at the nape of my neck had risen like antennae a half hour ago, my senses dialed past ten. The beef stew Addie had thrown together for dinner sat in my belly like a rock.

Most of the group stood in the circle of rugs and pillows in the center of the space. Addie was missing—she made preparations upstairs for the magical rite she was about to perform, binding us together in a low-level re-creation of the magic we'd used to invade the Order. The center rug had been laid out with a simple altar ahead of time—a small cauldron filled with rubbing alcohol and Epsom salts, a red candle, and a rough stone with a natural depression in the middle.

Charlie insisted that he didn't need anything fancy. He could do the magic we needed as easily as breathing.

I understood his point, and I felt the same way. I used my magic as a weapon, in survival situations, as a last resort. Most of the time, that meant quick and dirty, not with forethought or ceremony.

But I also got Addie's point. Practice mattered. Intention mattered.

If you had the time to properly prepare for a magical undertaking, you ought to take that time. Some of Addie's reasons had nothing to do with proper magical practice and everything to do with Charlie's arrested illness and the strangeness of our travel through the In-Between, with the group Charlie led arriving after me even though they'd stepped into the portal first.

Addie insisted we get fancy because we might need it.

While we waited, Sunday hovered at the far side of the altar, eyes on the side door to the house as the closest point of vulnerability. Beth backed her up. Charlie bowed to the funk happening with his health and magic and sat on a bright yellow pillow on the side closest to the stairs. Red hovered behind me.

The new arrivals, just back from trying to convince Corey's parents that she was where she was supposed to be, stood in front of me. Ben and Jess took in the story I'd told them, faces clouding.

Ben wore a dark gray hoodie over a white T-shirt and faded jeans. His blue wool hiking socks had a hole near his left big toe. He served as the unofficial leader among the kids. He'd been the first to welcome Faith into the fold when we'd moved to Portland. He was loyal and responsible and a lot older than his years. His long brown hair and even longer bangs hid half of his face, revealing one sharp eye and his meticulously groomed soul patch. His halo resembled a gray stone wall, and was just as impenetrable by magic. Ben was a shield—he could protect himself and anyone else who stood close enough.

His deep voice sounded a little nasal. He wiped his nose on his sleeve. Kid was coming down with a cold.

"It's too bad Faith has to stay in Texas," he said. "We could use her help here."

"Now that her magic is god-powered?" Jess asked. "Yeah. The ability to make an enemy explode in the blink of an eye would be hella useful right now. And with Corey not coming back either—I hope we don't need anyone who talks to ghosts."

Jess's comments about Faith's and Corey's abilities were real on their face, but this was about more than their magic. They were her friends, her team.

"They're okay," I said. "That's what matters. How did Corey's mom take the news?"

"Not well," Jess said.

Ben sighed. "She threatened to call my dad. She threatened to call Addie."

Jess was Addie's niece, and Watcher-in-training herself. Her halo looked like her aunt's—like a night full of stars. She'd twisted her dark, kinky curls into her favorite style, a loose bun on top of her head. Her favorite gold hoops dangled from her ears. She wore an olive green sweatshirt and black leggings. She'd shoved her feet into fuzzy frog slippers. At five feet tall, she was small but deadly.

"I don't blame her," Ben said. "I'd be out of my mind with worry, too. Good luck to her, getting a hold of my dad with his travel schedule. She's more likely to catch Addie, thank God. Anyway, we had to give her something."

"What?" I asked.

"We promised that Corey would call. And we had to give Corey's parents a phone number to call if they wanted."

"Whose number?" I asked.

Jess flashed a wry grin. "That guy, Malek. Snake Bite Tattoo?"

I had a hard time imagining Malek calming distraught parents. "He's gonna love that."

"Too bad." Ben folded his arms across his chest. His friends were his top priority—screw the serpent.

Once upon a time, she and Ben and Corey had placed protecting Faith at the top of their to-do list, going so far as to finding a hideout that I didn't know about. They'd wanted to keep her safe from harm by the Angel or any other comers. Faith no longer needed protecting, but they might.

"So, how does this time travel thing work?" Jess asked.

"I'm just playing my part," I said. "Your aunt is doing all the hard work."

"What are we supposed to do?" Ben asked.

"Right now, be ready to shield in case we need it, Ben," I said.

Jess leaned in to plant a kiss on Ben's cheek. "I'll see if my aunt needs help."

She made her way to the edge of the protections, disappearing through the curtain of magic and heading upstairs.

Ben looked over his shoulder, following her progress even after she faded from sight.

"You worried about her?" I asked.

He shook his head. "Just worried. It's like—my hackles are up. Like something's going to go wrong."

The hairs on the back of my neck spoke the same message. I'd refused to lie to Faith, and I wouldn't lie to her friends, either, or pretend everything was fine. "I have the same concern."

"You think something will go wrong with the time travel?" he asked.

"Maybe," I said.

He thought about it a little longer. "You think we're just waiting for some other shoe to drop?"

"What do you mean?" I asked.

"You know, bad shit happens so often. We could be waiting for the next bad thing, anticipating it, expecting it to happen. Maybe it's just that."

It was possible. But I didn't think so.

Before I could say that, Ben went on. "Or we're paranoid because someone is actually out to get us."

I laid a hand on his shoulder. "Just be ready if we need you?"

He nodded and wandered away to check in with Sunday and Beth, who were familiar faces, his gaze sweeping over Miguel and Charlie as he did. Charlie, the unknown quantity. A kid from another era. And Miguel, soaking up as much of Charlie and his magic as possible.

Red stepped in close behind me, threading his fingers through mine. "Tell me again that you'll be careful."

He didn't want me to travel without him, but he wouldn't say so outright. He knew I could take care of myself, but he worried.

"I'll be careful," I said. "It's a short trip."

"Find out what Luna knows."

"And bring her back—forward—with us."

He leaned in, planting a kiss on my cheek. "We'll be here."

The basement's protections opened to admit Addie, dressed in a robe that shimmered with stars as her halo did, her feet bare regardless of the chill. Jess swooped in behind her, still in her street clothes, but her halo had shifted—it held more stars than I'd ever seen within it, as if she'd kicked up her magic a notch.

Addie met my gaze. "You all ready?"

"Let's do it." I let my magic rise within me, filling my skin and spilling over into my own halo.

Addie moved to the rug in the center of the room and knelt. I made my way over to her and hunkered down at her left, and Red crouched at mine.

"Everybody," she said.

Sunday and Ben and Jess converged on us, with Beth reluctantly bringing up the rear. Charlie duckwalked over from his bright yellow perch, Miguel by his side. They were the first to reach for Addie and me, resting hands on our backs. The others crouched or bent, laying on hands, until the entire group connected.

"Take a deep breath," Addie said. "In for one, two, three, four. Hold for two, three, four. Exhale, two, three four. Three more of those."

We breathed in together, exhaled together, tuning our raggedy nerves to the same calm frequency.

When Addie spoke again, she did so softly and with an air of solid authority. "Now, take a full, deep breath and let go of anything you don't want to bring into this working with you—anxiety or worry, fear, judgment. Make a sound as you release it."

One more deep breath, as instructed, with a charged *ha!* as we breathed out.

"We're here," Addie said. "We've got each other. Most of us are close. We've been so close that our magic has mingled. We know what and how each other thinks and feels. We may not be bound thus magically right now, but we can call on our memory of that if we need to. May we be in the right place at the right time. May we do this working with clarity and courage. Amen."

"Amen," Red murmured.

Addie lit the red candle, a flame to light our way to Luna and back again.

"Light leads to light," Addie chanted.

Jess picked up the chant with her, their voices growing louder with each repetition, weaving into a harmony. The candle flame flared high and bright.

The time was right. We were ready. The group moved apart, but I could still see the fine, shimmering threads of magic that stretched among us.

The air around Charlie seemed to waver. I hoped that was his magic revving up and not some kind of trouble on the way.

Plenty could go wrong. We could end up in the wrong time. We could end up trapped in time if Charlie's magic failed—which was why Miguel had stuck so close to Charlie all afternoon and evening, and why he was going with us as backup.

We could have trouble finding Luna, or getting her to believe us when we told her she was in danger and that magic was real. If our arrival coincided with Gabriel's, they might not take kindly to our interference. If Pestilence was tracking Luna, and we ran into it—or if Pestilence showed up at the house while we were gone—

We'd considered the options. We'd talked them over. We had to risk going back for Luna.

Sunday would stay behind with Addie, Red, and the kids. Beth would act as Sunday's backup.

Addie pushed to her feet, turning to look at Charlie. "Ready?"

He nodded.

"We've got your back," she said.

"Thanks." He wiped his palms on his pants. "Join hands, thumbs to the left."

Miguel and I circled with Charlie and did what he asked. Touching Charlie felt like laying hands on a live electrical current. My hair stood on end, from the top of my head to the fine hairs on my arms.

My mind blanked. My lungs seized. My heart stuttered. It took a minute to be able to breathe again. For my heartbeat to settle. For words and images to suffuse my mind again.

"Close your eyes," he said. "Night, imagine Luna. Not how she died, but the way she looked and the way she moved. The sound of her voice. Everything she told you and showed you about her meeting with Gabriel."

I conjured all of those things about Luna, all of the pieces of her in my memory falling into place, living and breathing like the woman herself had once been.

"Got it," I said.

"Okay," Charlie said. "Now let go of the vision. Trust me, and let me steer."

I cleared my mind, conscious of only the flow of my magic and the shaky rise and fall of my breath, of the basement chill and Miguel's and Charlie's hands in mine. Then the floor disappeared from underfoot. My stomach shot into my throat. I fell.

I tightened my grip on Miguel and Charlie, but could no longer feel the shapes of their hands. I tumbled forward, my body spinning in a long arc, slowly at first and then gaining enough speed to cut the air.

The stench of sulfur filled my mouth. Heat licked the edges of my skin. I held my breath, knowing that we passed through the In-Between, knowing that if I inhaled, the heat would sear my lungs.

A heartbeat later, the spinning stopped abruptly. My feet settled on earth—or concrete. The perfume of rain filled the air, warring with the noxious fumes of car exhaust and the stink of alcohol-tinged vomit nearby.

I viscerally felt the urge to throw up myself. I swallowed hard.

My sense of Miguel and Charlie, and their hands in mine, returned slowly. They held on to me as tightly as I squeezed them—tight enough to cut off the circulation.

"We okay?" I asked.

Miguel let go, shaking like a dog, and breathed out a huge sigh. "Damn."

"You get used to it." Charlie gave my fingers a last pinch, then released me to crack his knuckles. "This look right, Night?"

Fine drizzle and dark skies. A sidewalk on the west side of the Willamette River. The ribbon of concrete called Naito Parkway stretched in front of us, bisected by a green esplanade. Across the road, a closed convenience store, its darkened windows watching us with disinterest.

The Broadway Bridge loomed above, its rust-colored metal casting shadows filled with foreboding. Behind us, apartment buildings loomed. The block looked and felt empty except for us, although I could hear a single set of boots clock with each step to the south, on the other side of the railroad tracks there, their owner not yet in sight.

Luna.

"I recognize it," I said. "This is the place where Gabriel ambushed Luna. We have a handful of minutes before he arrives."

Charlie nodded, spinning on his heel and breaking into a jog to intercept Luna. Miguel and I followed.

The Luna I caught sight of resembled the Luna I'd met physically— a tall, skinny, bundled-up woman passing through the puddled light of infrequent streetlamps. The strip of long hair that ran along the center of her scalp lifted in a gust of wind. The quick rhythm of her boots on the sidewalk wary.

She wasn't the same woman, though. No black-mirror halo here, just a normal, sweet, healthy silver glow. No magic. Not yet.

Luna glimpsed us in that moment, drawing her hands from her pockets. I caught the glint of metal in her right fist.

"Knife," I said.

Miguel marked the weapon. "Smart."

Luna stopped twenty feet away. Her voice drifted to us. "What do you want?"

Charlie slowed to a stop, his breath coming a little fast. "Hey. Remember me?"

She blinked at him. "You—what are you doing here?"

"I know I swore never to darken your door again," he said.

She nodded. "Because you're weird."

"But I'm here to repay the favor you granted me, Luna."

She cocked her head. "I saved your life."

He nodded.

She pressed her free hand to her chest. "I'm in danger. Real danger?"

"We need to go now," Charlie said. "Do you trust me?"

She shook her head, but her heart wasn't in the gesture. She lifted her chin, pointing toward Miguel and me. "Who're they?"

"Friends. Protection." Charlie reached for her hand. "Please."

She glanced down at the knife in her hand. "Protection from what?"

"Something that blade won't help with," he said.

She hesitated for a second that seemed to go on forever before she closed the knife and dropped it back into her pocket. She took Charlie's hand.

She hadn't taken much convincing. That had to be down to Charlie.

"Circle up now," he said.

Miguel and I took each other's hands. I reached for Luna.

She stared at my hand as if it weren't human at all—as if it were alien. Her eyes widened, and she met my gaze. "What are you?"

How did she know? How could she see? She had no magic. She was a normal, and normals never noticed anything about us.

We didn't have time for this—not now. "I'll tell you when we get where we're going."

She furrowed her brow. "Where's that?"

"Out of here before trouble comes," Miguel said. "Any minute now, a guy with a voice full of bells will walk up and dose you with magic so strong, you'll be dead by sunrise."

Luna's eyebrows climbed to her hairline. She tensed as if she intended to bolt, but she didn't move a muscle. "You're talking about the future."

Charlie nodded.

"That's impossible," Luna said.

"It should be," he said. "But it's not."

"You're talking about magic."

"Charlie is magic," Miguel said. "You knew that already."

Her mouth fell open. She was surprised, but not by Miguel's words. Something else had struck her.

"I hear bells," she said.

Gabriel, on the way. How far? "Faint or loud?"

"Faint," she said.

"Take our hands," Charlie said.

She did, but her grip was tentative. She wasn't sure about us. But the current than ran through our closed circuit took hold of her. It wouldn't allow her to let go.

A heartbeat later, the sidewalk dropped out from underneath us, flinging us through time.

Luna screamed.

The gong of bells filled the air, blotting out every other sound, pressing into my skin and working its way into my blood.

We spun forward in time, slicing through the sulfur-drenched In Between and landing, electric and dazed and deafened by Gabriel's roaring, ringing voice.

Concrete under our feet again—this time, indoors. The brightly colored pillows and rugs and strong protections that surrounded Addie's basement were all there, as were the people we'd left moments ago. Sunday guarded the side door, and Beth the other entrance to the space, closer to the staircase. Addie, Ben, and Jess had been leaning against the wall near Beth when we'd come through. They stood at attention now, eyes wide.

Red was closest to the center of the circle, hands shoved into the front pockets of his jeans as he paced. He met my gaze, green eyes piercing all the way to my depths. His grass-and-earth magic flared along our heart link. I felt his relief for a single second before he turned to the others in our party, checking to make sure that our appearances didn't lie.

All four of us had come through.

Charlie, looking worse for wear, his white shirt and brown trousers even more rumpled, his white skin extra pale and blotchy.

His golden hair hung in his eyes and his hands shook when he let go of us. His halo still looked like the shining sun, with no green tint, but its brightness had diminished.

Miguel ran his hands along the edges of his body as if he wasn't sure where he ended and the rest of the world began. His purple bruise of a halo expanded, helping him to take up more space, to stabilize.

Luna stared at them, and then at me. She trembled all over, so much so that I wrapped an arm around her and helped her sit on one of the pillows.

"Hey, Ben?" I called.

"Water?" he asked.

"Please," I said.

Luna grabbed my arms, fingers sinking deeply enough to drive bruises. "What the hell just happened?"

"Charlie brought us forward in time. This basement—this house—belongs to our friend, Addie." I hooked a thumb over my shoulder. "That's her, right there."

Luna spared Addie a quick glance. "Why does looking at her make my eyes hurt?"

Addie stepped forward. "What do you see?"

"Stars," Luna said.

Addie rushed toward us, kneeling beside me. "That's impossible. You'd have to have magic to see me that way."

Some normals had a certain amount of psychic ability, a trait passed down to them from one or both parents. At the Order, they'd taught us that this type of ability lingered in non-magical humans because their blood ancestors maintained a close connection with the world—or worlds—around them. They hadn't yet decided that nonhuman beings didn't exist, or weren't worthy of souls or love or intelligence.

Maybe Luna fit that bill. But I didn't think so.

I looked at her more closely. Her sweet silver halo began to shift before my eyes, darkening to a shiny black around the edges.

I tried to keep my voice even. "Luna, did you hear bells earlier in the night—before we found you?"

She nodded. "I was still at the bar, closing up after my shift. I kind of blacked out for a few minutes while I was mopping in the bathroom."

I closed my eyes.

"What?" she asked.

Addie sat back on her haunches, deflating as she exhaled. "These folks came to get you to stop you from encountering an archangel who planned to give you magic. They wanted to spare you from what's about to happen."

"I don't understand," Luna said. "What's about to happen?"

I turned my voice to the Angel. *There's no way to stop this?*

None, he said, as Beth came forward, her jade knife at the ready.

I held up a hand to stave her off.

"But we have the time now," Beth said. "Charlie got us the time."

I shook my head. "The Angel says it won't work."

Luna shook me, fingers still digging into my arms. "Tell me."

I took a deep breath and looked her in the eye. "Your body and soul can't handle the magic that you were given. It's only a matter of time before you—"

"Die," she said.

I nodded.

"How do you know?" she asked.

"Because it happened once before," I said.

She took in what I'd said. She scanned the faces of everyone assembled, and saw the truth in their eyes as well. Her gaze landed finally on Charlie.

"You said that you'd come to return the favor. To save my life."

The corners of his mouth turned down. "I'm sorry it didn't work. I was sure that it would. We all were."

"Thank you for trying," she said.

His mouth began to tremble.

Luna loosened her grip on me, allowing me to smooth her hair away from her face and brush my hands along the tops of her shoulders and down her arms. To give what comfort I could.

Even as I did, the last of the silver in her halo turned black, a shine rising to burnish its dark surface.

"Will it hurt?" she asked.

I kept my gaze locked on hers. "It was sudden before. Fast."

She took hold of my hands and twined her fingers with mine. "Why did this happen to me?"

What could I possibly tell her that would make sense?

"It's nothing you did," I said. "It's not your fault."

She shook her head. "But it's happening to me. That has to mean something."

"That's not necessarily true," I said.

"But you think it is."

I felt everyone's eyes on me, watching and waiting to see what I would say. What I would do. I felt Red's pulse through the heart link, and the love he sent. I took as much of that love as I could and let it infuse my voice and my eyes. I wanted Luna to see it. I need her to.

She was about to die in a stranger's basement, and she should know why if she could handle it. She should know that people cared about her.

"I do," I said.

She searched my face. "What does it mean?"

"There's a war," I said. "We're fighting it."

"With magic?" she asked.

I nodded. "There's a—I know how this sounds—Horseman of the Apocalypse who is searching for a human to possess. I think that human is supposed to be you."

Luna sucked in a breath. For a heartbeat, I wasn't sure whether she intended to laugh or cry or yell.

She did none of those things. Instead, she asked a question that assumed what we'd just told her was not preposterous. She asked as if she believed every word.

"Is that what you are? A Horseman of the Apocalypse?"

My mouth fell open. "I'm human. I have magic. I was born that way. But, yes, I am a vessel for a Horseman. He lives inside of me."

"Which one?" she asked.

"*La Muerte.*"

She tried on a grin that didn't touch her eyes. "For real?"

I nodded. "I'm so sorry that this is happening to you."

"Yeah," she said. "Me, too."

"Is there anyone you want us to call?" I asked.

She shook her head. "No. No one."

No family. No friends. Luna was all alone in the world. Holy hell.

She closed her eyes tightly. After a moment, she looked at me again. "Don't leave me?"

"I won't," I said. "That's a promise."

She let go of my hands, as if she knew that what was coming could hurt me in some way. She scooted back a few inches, far enough away to spare me and Addie, who hadn't moved so much as an inch—yet close enough to still feel near.

I had a question. I needed an answer. "Luna, in all of this, is there anything that feels familiar? Some thought that's come up that feels powerful?"

"Nothing," she said.

The voice that'd spoken in my dream had insisted that there should be.

Luna knows.

But whatever the woman might know, there was no time to discover it.

Her halo began to melt, and she flushed red with the heat gathering at her core. She locked her gaze with mine and didn't look away. She didn't even blink. She looked into me, and I into her, as the heat burst through her and she turned to ash for the second time today.

This time, it was Addie whose movement stirred the air enough to break apart what remained of Luna.

She turned to me, her face a mask of rage. "This won't stand."

"No," I said. "I won't allow it."

And I meant that, down to the marrow of my bones.

CHAPTER 8

ONE BY ONE, the others made their way out of the basement and up the stairs. Addie left first, taking Ben and Jess with her. Then Charlie, blinking away tears, with Beth at his side. With each departure, the space felt colder. The bright touches from the pillows and rugs seemed garish. The red candle still burned on the altar, a mockery of the magic we'd used it to create. Luna had gone up so fast and so utterly that the stench of her burning had lasted all of a minute. Now, the room smelled as if she'd never been there. Never existed at all.

Sunday hadn't moved from her station at the side door. Miguel had walked over to stand with her. They spoke in hushed tones. I couldn't hear a single word. I needed to stand up and meet them. We needed to go over what had happened. Strategize. Plan.

But I couldn't bring myself to leave the spot where I knelt. I couldn't take my eyes off of the altar. Like everything else in the vicinity, it was dusted with Luna's ashes.

Red hunkered down beside me in the space that Addie had occupied a few minutes ago. His shaggy hair hid his face. He locked his fingers together so tightly, his knuckles bleached.

"You want to go up?" he asked.

I shook my head. The altar held all the elements I needed.

He tucked his hair behind his ear, turning to meet my gaze. "You need some time? Or are you and Miguel gonna try again?"

We could. I didn't know whether that would turn out any better. I didn't understand time the way Charlie did, but even Charlie's expertise might not be enough.

What I'd said to Michael in the dream still held. Time was the enemy.

"Michael told me that Gabriel didn't make mistakes," I said. "I don't believe archangels are all-powerful. I want to believe that someone or something ought to be able to undo what Gabriel's done. Wanting it didn't make it real."

He considered that. "It's a good thought, undoing what Gabriel did. I haven't got the first clue how we go about doing that. We need someone with more depth of angel knowledge than I've got."

"That's not me, unfortunately."

"Even with the Angel of Death in there?"

I nodded. "Nothing he could do for Luna. And he's not adding anything to this conversation. So either he's got his marching orders and won't color outside the lines, or—"

"Or he can't help," Red said.

I nodded.

"Her soul is gone, too," he said. "Luna's soul. Burned away with the rest of her, just like before. I still can't explain it. Doesn't make any sense."

"It's not right."

"No," he said. "It's not."

"She's important. She's part of this—whatever this is. With the Horseman."

"Yeah," he said. "I know you've been thinking she might be the Horseman's vessel. You ever think she might've been the one to help you stop him?"

"It hadn't occurred to me. No."

"Single-minded," he said. "You want me to stay?"

I didn't want him to go, but it might be easier if he did. "Yes."

"Sounds conditional."

"You're not gonna like what I have in mind."

"Why don't you let me be the judge of that?"

I couldn't quite bring myself to smile. He read it in me all the same.

"So," he said. "What are we up to?"

I stood up slowly, every muscle aching from having been tensed so tightly. Red followed suit. Sunday and Miguel left off their conversation and made their way over to us.

Sunday slipped her fingers into her back pockets. "You couldn't leave the altar. I can only think of one thing you might want to use it for."

Miguel folded his arms across his chest. "Which asshole are we summoning?"

No question about whether we should. No platitudes. They were all in. "Gabriel. Let's see whether they're any better than Michael at showing up when they're needed."

Red opened his mouth to say something, but no words flowed out. He looked as if he'd been hit by a bucket of cold water.

"Is this what y'all do when I'm not around?" he asked.

Miguel answered. "Pretty much."

Red threaded his fingers again, this time resting them on top of his head. "Okay. How can I help?"

"Keep an eye," I said. "Make sure we've got the right archangel."

"What are you gonna do?" he asked.

I held out a hand. "Need a blade."

Sunday slapped the hilt of her knife into my palm.

The Angel's voice echoed inside my head. *You want my help?*

What help are you prepared to give? I asked.

Whatever will keep you safe, he said.

I'm not interested in safety. I'm interested in getting to the bottom of this. In figuring out how to stop the rest of the Horsemen from taking vessels. Because, once they do, there will be no stopping it.

The Apocalypse. The end of everything.

Consider your intention. Know that this could go terribly wrong, he said.

What if it goes right?

The odds are against that.

What odds? I asked.

The Angel froze me in place, taking control of my body faster than I could even hope to resist. *I could make you stop.*

He could. He'd proved time and again that he could make me do or see whatever he wanted. But he'd never done so except in service of the greater goal. He'd never forced me from a chosen path. He'd never acted out of spite, or to preserve his authority. I didn't think he'd start now.

You could, but you won't, I said. *Why not?*

We're a team, he said. *We're together or we are not at all. Your human existence tethers me to your world. You make it possible for me to walk here. To influence. To act. I will never know what it's like to be human, but you do, Night. You know in your heart.*

My heart. The seat of my magic, among other precious things.

Then let me go, I said.

In the space of a breath, I could move again. Speak again.

I closed my eyes, reaching out to touch the spirit of the house. I showed it what I intended to do. It indicated that it would open the way for my magical working. It would also have to tell Addie immediately.

Addie might not agree with what I had in mind. I had no way to know without requesting her permission, and I was in no mood to ask.

Quick and dirty magic would serve—this time, the same magic Malek and I had used in creating the ink that arrested Charlie's illness. Magical properties and signatures carried within the blood.

I sliced open the meat of my palm, allowing the blood to fall, mingling with the red candle's flame and the ashes that had once been Luna.

Red sucked in a breath. "Holy shit, Night."

In this case, I wasn't praying for healing. I sent out a call, and with the blood made damn sure that Gabriel knew who'd sent it. I breathed in, drawing in the taste and scent of copper. I exhaled, heart racing.

The side door that Sunday had been guarding began to glow

around the edges, the light that appeared behind it bright enough to blind. The wood shook inside the frame, the hardware rattling. Then the lock turned with a click that echoed against the concrete floor and walls and the door swung open on squealing hinges.

The light flashed so strongly that for a hot minute I had to shut my eyes, before it coalesced into a figure walking toward us. Their perfume of freshly fallen snow overpowered the copper of my blood. They looked human, except they shone like polished gold. Their eyes were made of light.

I'd seen Gabriel through Luna's eyes, through her memory. It didn't compare to being in the same room with them.

Gabriel wore the faded, skinny jeans and white cable-knit sweater I'd seen in Luna's memory. Their brown leather boots made no sound on the basement floor—but left a trail of footprints that glowed like banked coals. Their golden hair stuck out in every direction. They didn't look male, and they didn't tend toward female, either. I'd never seen a being so completely androgynous.

When they spoke, the sound of ringing bells filled the room—so loudly, I had to fight the urge to clap my hands over my ears.

"You," they said. "You've got some cheek."

I'd been called all kinds of things before, but no one had ever called me cheeky. "I asked. You came."

"Curiosity," they said.

Bullshit. "Why did you dose Luna with magic?"

"Skipping the small talk," Gabriel said. "I *gifted* her to bring her here. To you."

"She died," I said. "Twice."

They shrugged. "Going back in time as you did set off a kind of magical chain reaction. You're caught in it now, although you don't seem to realize that yet. You'll have to see it through if you want to find out what Luna knows."

"How did you know about that? Are you the voice inside my head?"

Gabriel shook their head. "You have plenty of voices without adding mine to the mix. How I came to glean that bit of knowledge isn't important. What you do from this moment on is. Watch over her, Night. If she dies a third time, all will be lost."

"The hell does that mean?"

The archangel gave no answer to the question. "Let me save you another trip."

Gabriel blew out a long breath like a breeze on a hot day, warm and crackling with life and promise. That breath reached all the way to me in the space of a single heartbeat. It stirred the bloody ashes at my feet. It brushed them with magic deeper than I'd ever encountered.

The archangel's polished gold flashed brighter than before, bleeding the room and everyone in it of color, leaving us all black and white. When the light had faded, Gabriel was gone.

The ashes still quivered with the archangel's breath—no, more than that.

They began to coalesce as if drawn together by a magnetic force—the strength of Gabriel's magic. They reassembled themselves into human form, carrying with them the blood I'd allowed to fall—blood tinged with Michael's power, and the Angel of Death's as well.

Fire ignited on their surface, traveling from the outside in. When the flames reached the core, my vision went gray. I couldn't see at all.

I blinked furiously. It didn't help. The rush of my blood filled my ears. My heart raced, beating so fast I thought it might give out.

As suddenly as the sound and fury had taken over, they subsided. I blinked again.

My vision came clear, color flooding in. In front of me, where her ashes had once peppered the concrete, sat Luna. Living and breathing and shaking like a whole forest of leaves in a high wind. Buck naked— the fire had burned her clothes, and Gabriel's magic hadn't recreated them along with their owner.

Red moved first, stripping off his T-shirt and handing it to Luna. That was kind enough, but she needed more clothing than that, cold as she seemed.

Sunday echoed my thoughts and headed for the washer and dryer. "There's a load of blankets that finished drying this afternoon. I don't think anyone's folded them yet."

I knelt in front of Luna, taking her by the arms as she'd done to me before. It took her a moment to meet my gaze.

Her teeth chattered. "Night."

I nodded.

"I died."

"Yes," I said.

"How am I here?"

"Gabriel."

"They brought me back?" she asked.

"They did, but if you want to know why or how, I'm not sure. They said some things that didn't make a lot of sense. We need to figure it out."

Sunday squatted behind her, wrapping her in a white down comforter. "That better?"

Luna nodded, giving me a second to let go so that she could grab the edges of the comforter and draw them tight.

"Thanks," she said. "So, what now?"

The protections opened to admit Addie, still in her ritual robe. Though stars in her halo shone with an angry fire, she schooled her expression. She carried a mug in hand, the comforting scent of hot cocoa steaming forth.

She flavored her voice with a little sarcasm. "We can't get rid of you, can we?"

Luna glanced at her, lips curving into the wisp of a grin. "No," she said. "Sorry."

Addie handed me the mug, and I passed it on to Luna.

She looked into its chocolaty depths. "Marshmallows?"

"Only the best for those of us who've died twice."

Luna took a small sip, and then a gulp. The more hot chocolate she drank, the more present she seemed. The drink grounded her back into her body, into the here and now.

Addie seemed satisfied with what she saw. "Red, Sunday, Miguel— you all take Luna upstairs and find her something to wear? We can meet in the kitchen in a while. I'll put something together for us."

Red looked at me, raising a brow.

I shrugged. If Addie wanted to be pissed at someone, she should be pissed at me. If she had something to say about it outside of the others' earshot, I was fine with that. I could take it.

He offered a hand to Luna. She let him help her to her feet and followed him through the protections, Sunday and Miguel at their heels.

Addie stared at me.

I folded my arms across my chest and waited.

She pitched her voice at a whisper. I got the impression that if she hadn't, she'd have yelled her throat raw.

"Give me your hand," she said.

She meant the one I'd cut. I did what she asked.

She pulled a piece of gauze and a red bandana from her pocket. She slapped on the gauze and fixed it with the bandana, pulling the cloth tight enough to make me wince. I felt sure that she wanted me to hurt. Her next words bore that out.

"You infuriate me, Night."

"Because I called Gabriel without your permission?"

She took a step toward me. The silver rims of her glasses twinkled under the overhead light. "Also, you're stupid."

"I've got this wrong," I said. "You're angry because I didn't ask you to help."

"Damn right. And don't tell me it was impulse that you summoned Gabriel. You meant to do it from the minute Luna passed."

"I meant to do something," I said. "I didn't overthink it."

She narrowed her eyes, searching my face. After a moment, she sighed. "You do that again and I'll kick your ass."

I might be the trained Order operative, but I wouldn't underestimate her determination—or her magical ability to reweave the fabric of the universe.

She took my silence as understanding. "You will tell me every single thing you did to call Gabriel to you, and you will tell me every single thing they did and said."

I recounted every detail, watching her take in the story and process it on the fly.

"We need to talk with Luna," she said. "Whatever she knows, it's possible it's not in her conscious mind. It could be something hidden. Something only her subconscious knows. Or a repressed memory."

Discovering new information about my life had meant having to reevaluate who I was and why, more than once. I didn't wish that on anyone. "For her sake, I hope not."

Addie's face softened. "It's not easy, is it?"

I shook my head.

"We should do this thing in as small a group as possible," I said. "I don't want Luna feeling like she's being interrogated by a crowd."

"As long as I'm one of the group, Night."

"I wouldn't dream of it any other way," I said.

"Yes, you would." She thought for a moment. "You and I. And Red should be the third."

"Because he sees."

"And because of the effect he has on people. He calms them. They know he sees who they are and that he genuinely cares about them. That he'll protect them. It's a rare gift."

"Beth says he's the embodied sacred heart."

Addie's eyes widened. "I hadn't thought of it that way."

"That's two of us."

"What do you think?"

"I don't know," I said. "But I haven't met anyone like him. No one else who can do what he can."

"That's true of all magicians. We're all one of a kind—except chameleons."

I nodded. "Whatever he's got, I'm glad we've got him."

"I'm glad you've got him, Night." She looked me up and down. "I take it back about your being stupid."

"No, you don't," I said.

She cracked a weary smile.

I followed her out, peering over my shoulder before I stepped through the shielding.

The basement looked as if it had never held a dying woman or her ashes, or been stained with my blood. The archangel had left a sign of their presence, however.

The footprints burned into the concrete, black as coal.

Gabriel had warned that all might be lost if we didn't find a way to keep Luna alive. I didn't want to know what they meant by that, but I feared I would find out—sooner rather than later.

I slipped through the shielding and took the stairs two at a time, emerging from the basement underworld and stepping into the human world of bustling life. Sunday had taken charge of the kitchen, barking orders at Beth and Miguel. I smelled bacon again, and had to laugh—Sunday cooked breakfast again because she hardly knew how to cook anything else. She didn't do domesticity.

Addie sat down beside Luna on the sofa nearest the door, where Charlie had slept earlier. Luna's shaking had settled a little, though she still looked chilled and little pale. She wore Addie's purple sweatshirt and a pair of black leggings, black wool socks on her feet. Sunday or someone else had refilled her cocoa. She sipped quietly.

She didn't look quite right, and not because she was still in shock. Her healthy human halo had no defined borders. The edges were tattered, undulating like a torn flag in high wind.

I'd never seen a halo like that. I didn't know how to read it. If I had access to Luna's mind, I might be able to decipher it.

I looked at Addie. She shook her head, the movement so small Luna didn't pick it up. The message was clear: not yet.

She was right, of course—so I focused on the one other thing that seemed clear from a detailed look at Luna. The magic that Gabriel had originally dosed her with, the magic that had incinerated her from the inside out, remained. Either Gabriel had resurrected it along with her physical body or he'd gifted her with it again as she reconstituted.

This time, it didn't appear to harm her. She didn't have the magical feel of someone ready to explode or implode. She felt stable.

How could that be possible?

I needed to ask that question and more, but I needed Red's full attention focused on Luna first. I needed his non-invasive, compassionate soul-reading skills.

He knelt beside the hearth, building a fire, adding a last log as new flames flickered and rose. He wiped his hands on his jeans as he pushed to his feet.

I sat on the sofa opposite Addie and Luna. He settled in beside me.

Addie broke the ice. "This is unprecedented."

Luna frowned. "Resurrecting the dead?"

"No," Addie said. "That's definitely happened before. You feel any different than you did prior to—"

"Dying?"

Addie nodded.

"No," Luna said.

Red stroked his mustache, opening his mouth, hesitating to speak. "Nothing different at all? Nothing missing?"

Luna narrowed her eyes. "Please just tell me what it is."

He swallowed hard. "Near as I can tell, your soul is missing."

She stared at him.

I stared at him, too. I couldn't see that, not without entering her mind. But he could read hearts and souls, and if he said her soul was gone, it was goddamn gone.

"Your soul," he said again. "When you died, it burned with you. When Gabriel brought you back, he brought your body back, but your soul didn't come along with it. I think—I think it was destroyed."

"What?" she asked.

"I'm sorry," he said. "I don't know how else to describe it."

She looked at the hot chocolate in her mug. "Addie, do you have anything stronger than this?"

Addie shoved off the sofa. "Scotch or bourbon?"

"Scotch," Luna said.

Addie headed for a built-in cabinet in the corner, bringing back four glasses and a half full bottle of Highland single malt. She poured generously for all of us, with an extra finger of whisky for Luna, who took a huge sip, eyes closed as the fiery stuff flowed down her throat. The warmth it brought colored not only her cheeks, but her halo— golden sparks appeared amidst the tatters.

She looked at Red again. "Is my soul still gone?"

He nodded.

"What does that mean?" she asked.

"I wish I knew." He glanced at me. "Does the Order have any lore around losing a soul?"

"Not that they told me," I said.

Addie sipped her drink. "The Watchers have some. It's not detailed —most of the old lore is written in metaphors and requires that you already know what you're looking for, specifically."

"You had a reason to look for this lore?" I asked.

"I did," she said firmly, closing the door on that line of conversation. "What's relevant here is that a person without a soul is open to possession."

Luna sucked in a breath. "Jesus Christ. Possession—the hell does that mean?"

Addie laid a hand on her knee, more to hold her in place than to comfort. "It means that if a powerful enough spirit wanted to, they could walk right into your body, shove your consciousness to the back room, and lock the door. They'd be in charge then, wearing your body like a Luna suit, doing whatever they wanted with it."

Luna downed the rest of her whisky in one swallow. "That's like something out of a horror movie."

Addie poured her two more fingers. "This isn't a movie, Luna. This is your life."

Luna blinked, staving off sudden tears. "What if I don't want it?"

"It's too bad," Addie said. "Gabriel took that choice away from you."

"So did you. You could've left me dead and gone. Instead you traveled through time to get me before he could."

"To save you," Red said.

She looked him in the eye. "Do I look saved?"

He let her gaze bore into him, refusing to look away. "You look like a person whose life has just been turned upside down."

"Whose life has ended," she said.

"Only if you give up," I countered.

She tightened the grip on her glass. "Give up on what, Night? What am I supposed to hope for now?"

"That you have enough—that you *are* enough—to take on the fate Gabriel pushed on you."

"I'm not there yet," she said. "I might never get there. I don't do any of the stuff other people seem to do so effortlessly—I don't laugh in the face of danger. I don't pull on my big girl panties or buck up and suit up. I run. I hide."

"I get that," I said.

"You? You're some kind of trained military type, aren't you?"

"Magical assassin," I said.

"Magical assassin? For fuck's sake." She took another sip of her drink. "You have the skill here, not me. You probably run to danger instead of away from it."

Red sighed. "You're not wrong."

"There came a time when I had a choice to make—whether I wanted to stay with the people who trained me and continue to commit atrocities in their name. I took the girl who they'd sent me to kill and went underground. I raised the girl as my daughter. We hid from them for years and, when they got close, we ran. They were too powerful, and I had something precious to protect."

"That's admirable and honorable, or whatever—really, it is. But you did it for your daughter, not for yourself. There's a word for that. Selfless—self-sacrifice. I don't have that. You need to listen to me when I say that and believe me."

"Doesn't matter what I believe," I said. "You believe it. That's all that matters here."

She shook her head. After a moment, she wiped her eyes with the heel of her hand. "What else does it mean—having no soul? What am I if I don't have one? I can still think. I still feel."

"You're conscious," Addie said. "Consciousness—in possession of awakeness and awareness—is what you have when you're first born. Every infant has those things. A soul is built as we grow into ourselves. As we live, gaining experience, making decisions that shape the course of our lives. The soul is hard-earned. It's what connects us to the divine, however you might see divinity. It's the part of us that is divine."

"So I'm what, then—empty?" Luna asked.

I knew what it meant to have my soul annihilated. I knew what emptiness felt like. The hollow inside of me had never been the important thing, the thing that kept me up at night, staring at the ceiling. When I could sleep, it hadn't mattered much whether I would wake in the morning. I cared about one thing, and one thing only.

The small spark inside all of that emptiness. It lived and breathed and it wanted. It longed for what it had lost.

That longing drove me through every single moment until my new soul had been forged.

"What do you want?" I asked.

"Besides for this to be a bad dream?" she asked.

"What do you want?" I asked again. "If you had one wish, and someone could make it come true, what would it be?"

She shrugged.

Maybe she couldn't feel the desire yet. Maybe the shock of everything that had happened to her was still too new, too overpowering.

Finally, she asked, "Is there a way to get my soul back?"

"Maybe," I said.

"But you don't know for sure."

I could count the things I knew for sure on one hand. "There's not a one-size-fits-all fix for this. It's all nuance."

"You're making this shit up as you go along," she said.

I nodded.

She took a deep breath. "You obviously want me to do something. Want to tell me what it is?"

"It's not a to-do," I said. "It's a situation. We think the reason Gabriel gave you magic is because you have a part to play in our fight."

"The end of the world," she said.

I furrowed my brow. "We didn't talk about that before you died this time, but we did the first time."

"I remember," she said. "I don't know how, but I do."

Gabriel had talked about a magical chain reaction that we were caught in. It made sense that her remembering would be part of that. Her personal boundaries were wide open without her soul. Maybe that contributed to her remembering.

There was another, more worrisome explanation that had to do with time.

She'd been manhandled by an archangel. She'd died twice and been brought back to life. She'd been plucked from one point in the timestream and brought to another. What if her sense of time had become jumbled? What if she had access to the timestream in a way that none of us but Charlie had?

"I want to bring Charlie in on this conversation," I said.

Luna nodded. "Yes."

Red stood. "I'll get him."

"Thank you," Addie said.

He headed toward the kitchen.

Luna sipped her whisky. "What part do I play?"

"You know about the Angel I carry inside of me?" I asked.

"Yeah," she said. "The Angel of Death, right?"

I leaned forward, resting my elbows on my knees, and steepled my fingers. "He's a Horseman of the Apocalypse."

"Right," she said. "Because it's the end of the world. Okay. Catching up. What does that have to do with me?"

"There's another Horseman in town," I said. "He's a spirit right now. No body. He won't be able to walk and act in our world—at least not completely—without a human vessel to slip into."

Her eyes widened. "Oh, hell no."

Addie squeezed her knee. "Sorry, Luna."

"That's not something you can apologize for. And can you take your hand off of me?"

Addie let go of her. "Take your missing soul and the lore around possession. Add in a disembodied Horseman looking for a human vessel. We have to do the math. You're the logical candidate."

Luna pressed her lips together. "Which Horseman?"

Shoes squeaked on the hardwood behind us. Red returning with

Charlie. They brought the scent of roasting potatoes with them—Sunday crafting a monumental breakfast for dinner.

I glanced over my shoulder at them. Charlie's color had shaded toward green, as if the soul-deep sickness he'd contracted was making a comeback. Red planted his feet wide, hands curling into fists. He looked at Luna as if he'd seen a ghost—or something much, much worse.

"You know which Horseman," he said.

Luna set her drink down on the coffee table, drumming her fingertips on the oak. "You people have hit me with enough bullshit for one evening, don't you think?"

Anger had overtaken shock. Not too soon. Not unbelievable. But the tone in Luna's voice didn't sound true. The magical wind in her tattered halo picked up to storm strength.

My magic rose, bursting from the seams of my skin.

It knew what my conscious mind hadn't yet sensed. It fought against my control, wanting—needing—to launch.

I let it fly.

CHAPTER 9

MY MAGIC KNIFED INTO Luna before she could raise defenses. The inside of her mind looked nothing like it had before. Gone were the memories of her walk home from her bar shift, of her first encounter with Gabriel. In their place, a hum of distinctly non-human energy, the buzz like a swarm of wasps, stingers at the ready.

The Angel's wings fluttered inside my chest. His icy magic rose to join mine, chilling my blood and slowing my heart, frosting my skin and hair. We gripped the intruder's spirit tight, our magical hands wrapped around its throat. It struggled against the hold, but didn't have the power to break it.

I rifled through its memories, grasping one of its arrival in Portland earlier tonight, the wind and rain wrapping it in loving arms, drawing it to Addie's yellow two-story house atop a steep yard set with rosemary and lavender to ward against evil. Minor magic, that. Not nearly enough to drive it away.

It climbed the steps and paced the wide porch, its movement gently rocking the creaking wood chairs and frightening away the big black-and-white tomcat who slept on the railing. Holiday lights strung overhead shone bravely against the dark. The sweet scent of life—of cooked meals, perfume, friendship, dreams, tears, and laughter—permeated the air, enticing.

To be alive was the best thing.

The spirit could look through the windows. Study the occupants. But it couldn't enter. Not with the house spirit guarding the place and the Watchers inside.

The flashing colored lights of the tree in the corner of the dining room hypnotized. A boy slept on the sofa that faced away from the door, but the spirit recognized him from a previous encounter in another time.

The boy didn't have the juice to hold the spirit. Too bad—the boy's time magic held endless possibility. The idea of being able to travel back or forward in time, to be able to search for the what it wanted more than anything—but the boy couldn't hold it. The boy was not the promised vessel. There would be another.

It knew that deep in its magical heart, just as it knew there would be an opening in the protections that wrapped the house and kept it safe and free from intrusion.

To be on the outside looking in—that sliced at an old wound that had scabbed over, but never fully healed. The sleeping boy felt safe enough to let go of his conscious awareness in the company of others. The blankets he slept beneath spoke of the care of others.

That had to be an illusion. It could not exist. If it were real, Pestilence would have experienced it in all of the millennia since creation.

Pestilence's heart hardened as it looked at the boy, glad of the soul sickness it had imparted.

A spell had been woven into the sickness to stave off its worst effects, at least for a time. Pestilence recognized the serpent's signature in the magic. Powerful stuff. But not powerful enough to hold the sickness at bay forever.

The boy's connections with others would wither and die before he did. It was only a matter of time. That was how it should be. That was the best thing.

In that moment, the protections withdrew, the house spirit drawn away entirely, underground.

The spirit slipped into the house, flowing through the cracks between the door and the frame. It sensed power in the bowels of the house and raced for it, passing beyond the basement door, weaving around the magical humans who climbed the stairs, disguising itself in the aftermath of a magical death that had left the humans disheartened and oblivious to anything but the pain in their hearts.

The spirit knew that kind of pain. It knew intimately.

A handful of humans remained in the basement. One Order operative—the spirit would know an Order operative anywhere—and one who also smelled of the Order, but whose magic had been remade into something mutable. A chameleon.

The third, a man whose heart blazed like a fire, who smelled of growing things and earth. If he'd looked in the spirit's direction right then and there, he'd have seen it. But the man didn't look. He focused his attention on his mate—the last of the humans, who wasn't entirely human at all.

She held a knife in her hand, and she intended to use it.

She smelled like death. Like Death.

The Angel of Death.

The thoughts echoed in its—my head. It had recognized the Angel inside of me as its kin. As a brother. The Angel recognized it as well.

I withdrew my magic just enough to speak with the Horseman using my out-loud voice, and for it to answer in kind, so that the others in the room could hear the conversation.

"Pestilence," I said.

It spoke in Luna's voice, but no longer sounded like her. Its voice had an alien edge to it, something inhuman. It had never been human. No need to pretend any longer.

"I don't like that name," it said.

"What would you prefer I call you?" I asked.

"Luna," it said.

"That's the name of the human you've possessed. It's not yours."

Pestilence shrugged. "Why are you and your vessel holding me, brother?"

The Angel spoke through me. He asked a question—not one I expected.

The depth and cold in his voice reverberated in my bones. "What is your intention?"

"It's our time," Luna said. "I am here."

That was all. It was that simple. The time for the Horsemen to walk the worlds had come. Except I knew from what I'd seen in the Horseman's mind that it hadn't told the whole story. Something was missing. The thoughts Pestilence had as it waited for an opening to enter the house spoke of hatred—and longing. For what?

We were connected. It heard my thoughts as clearly as if I'd spoken them aloud.

"That is mine alone," it said. "We share many things, Death and I, but not that."

Were we really having a conversation about privacy? This was crazy.

I held its gaze, but my question was for the Angel alone. "Can we send it away?"

"No," the Angel said.

One word. So many shades of meaning.

We had more power than Pestilence and Luna, but we could not banish them. As a practicality, it would never work.

If Pestilence didn't find a properly prepared vessel in Luna, it would be forced to find one elsewhere. Someone else's life turned inside out, suffering.

Here, we had a chance to influence what it chose to do.

Pestilence's voice sliced into my thoughts. "Why would you want to send me away, brother?"

The Angel answered. "My vessel did not understand. She does now."

I did understand—and I hated it. I'd only wanted to save Luna. Instead, I'd served her up to a Horseman.

She had no soul. She had no hope. She and Pestilence would bring the kind of sickness that no one could cure to the whole mother-fucking human world, not to mention the other worlds, and the Angel was telling me the best outcome involved our influencing their choices?

The Angel's edges inside of me felt razor sharp—a warning not to push.

I wanted to scream until I ripped my throat raw.

Pestilence smiled at me. The Horseman meant it to be soft. Reassuring. It was neither. "I won't harm my vessel."

I took little comfort in that. I felt sure that the human Luna took none, trapped as she was in whatever corner of her mind the Horseman had locked her.

We couldn't hold Pestilence forever. We would have to let go sooner rather than later.

I pitched my voice to carry. "Charlie?"

He stepped into my line of sight.

"Can you take a look at the Horseman and tell me what you see?" I asked.

He eyed her closely. "Horseman, when did Gabriel first find Luna and gift her with magic?"

It looked at him as if it didn't understand the question.

"How long ago did it happen?" he asked.

It blinked slowly. "It's happening now."

I held my breath, wondering at that answer, but I heard no lie in it.

"What about when Luna died—the second time?" Charlie asked. "When did that happen?"

"Now," it said, as if the answer was obvious.

"Holy wow," he said.

La Muerte's edges softened. "You are broken," he said. "You will stay with us."

Pestilence nodded. "We belong together. We will always be together, brother. We swore at the beginning. Never forget."

What is it talking about? I asked the Angel, silently.

An old promise made before the dawn of time. A wicked vow we swore together, the four of us. An oath that we never should have made.

The Angel spoke aloud. "You forget that I've never been locked away from this world—not like you and the others. I know now what I didn't know then. I've learned."

"Learned," Pestilence whispered. "Fate has been your teacher?"

The Angel shook its head. "Not fate. Life."

For the space of a heartbeat, Pestilence drew a deep breath, all of its—and Luna's—molecules seeming to expand with the inhalation and to contract again as it exhaled. The air around it seemed to expand and shrink, dislocated and disoriented like a reflection in a funhouse mirror.

Pestilence met my gaze. Pestilence, Horseman of the Apocalypse, bent on finding something lost and infecting the world with soul sickness. Broken, with no sense of time. No perspective.

For a split second, the eyes changed. I swore that the being who looked at me through them was Luna herself—surprise and fear wild in her eyes. She opened her mouth. One word fell out.

"Night?"

I reached for her.

She—and the Horseman—broke the Angel's and my hold with a tearing sound that shuddered all the way to our core.

They disappeared in a rush of air that knocked her whisky glass from the table and onto the floor, where it shattered into dozens of shards. The depression in the cushion where she'd sat a moment ago remained, as did a trace of her scent—fire and ash and archangel's breath.

Where? I asked the Angel. *Where did they go?*

Not where, he said. *When. They dove into the past.*

Luna's past? The Horseman's?

No answer. He didn't know—or, if he did, he couldn't explain in terms I'd understand. *La Muerte* was no master of time. He was a master of death.

Charlie would know. Charlie and I could go after the Horseman— now, before it hurt anyone else. I opened my mouth to say so, but Addie whispered into the silence.

"Night?"

I blinked, focusing on her.

Sweat had bloomed on her forehead, but not from the heat of the fire.

"Addie, what's wrong?" I asked—although halfway through the question, I knew the answer.

Pestilence had infected her with the same soul sickness it had given Charlie.

I shot out of my seat, gaze grazing Charlie's and then Red's. He didn't appear any worse for wear. I tugged on the heart link, searching for damage that might not yet be visible. His heartbeat was strong. His body, healthy. He sent a barrage of emotion through the link. Love— followed by fear.

Maybe the Horseman had infected only Addie. Maybe not.

"I'll check the others," he said, already turning to run for the kitchen.

I needed to know that everyone was safe. I needed to contain the threat that Pestilence posed.

I felt for the house spirit—and found it stunned and overwhelmed, but marshaling its magical energies to protect the structure and everyone within.

"Night!" Red called.

I looked to Charlie. "Stay with Addie."

He nodded.

I ran toward Red, who'd wrapped his arm around Sunday, keeping her on her feet as he walked her toward the kitchen table and poured her into the nearest empty chair. The others filled the rest of the seats, every one of them sweating and turning pale and feverish.

Ben and Jess, huddled together, his stone-gray halo shielding them both. Miguel, his face not quite his own as it shifted to reflect the last few appearances he'd mimicked, including mine. The purple in his halo had bleached to lavender. And Sunday, the scar on her lip and the dark blue of her eyes the only color in her complexion. She bent forward, resting her head in her hands, looking as if she might throw up any second.

"Where's Beth?" I asked.

The back door slammed open. Rain and wind and the dark rushed inside—and so did Beth, eyes fierce behind the black frames of her glasses, her orange and black halo writhing. Streams of water slid down her raincoat and dripped onto the tile.

"I felt something happen," she said.

Red held up a hand—a signal for her to stay back.

"The hell is going on?" she asked.

"Pestilence," he said. "You don't look sick."

"I feel fine," she said. "What the—Pestilence got everyone?"

I met her gaze. "Everyone except Red and me. And you."

"I was outside."

I shook my head. "You came into contact with it in the basement. It had already possessed Luna. Best assumption is that if you were going to get sick, you'd be sick. The house spirit is depleted. We're vulnerable. Secure the house. Do whatever you need to."

"On it." She hurried out into the rain, presumably to check the perimeter.

I knelt beside Red, in front of Sunday, and took her hands in mine.

She struggled to sit up tall, and to focus her eyes enough to look at me.

"Damn thing got me before I could fight back," she said. "It was like a—like a ghost. Human-shaped. Transparent. Cold. It breezed through the kitchen. Passed through us one by one. Pestilence has Luna?"

I nodded.

"You kill it?" she asked.

"It got away," I said. "It has access to the timestream."

"Seriously?" She swallowed hard.

I slid over to the under-counter cabinets, grabbed a pot from Addie's cooking stash, and passed it to Red. He shoved it into Sunday's lap.

"Just in case," he said.

"I don't need a babysitter," she said. "I need to fight."

"You're sick, Sunday," Red said. "Your soul is sick. You're not in any shape to fight."

"Fuck you, Jennings."

"Not today," he said.

My need to scream filled up my flesh and blood and bones, searing the edges of my skin, throbbing in time with the beat of my heart. I gritted my teeth and clenched my fists to keep it at bay. It was all I could do.

These were my people. My family.

I looked at all of them. At the way the soul sickness had stolen their vitality immediately. It would get worse for them until the sickness killed them. There was no cure for it, only magic that could buy time.

Beth stepped through the back door again. "I've warded us. We're set out there."

Beth's wards would keep us invisible from magical sight, protected from all comers.

"Good," I said. "You bring your tattoo works in that backpack of yours?"

"Yeah," she said. "Be prepared."

"Get 'em."

She blew past me in a blur.

I shut the back door tightly and locked it, then grabbed a blade from Addie's knife drawer and turned off the burners under the bacon and potatoes.

"You're going to ruin the food," Sunday said.

"I'll buy you a goddamn meal," I said. "Try not to die on me before I get around to it."

In the seat beside hers, Miguel leaned back, lifting the front legs of the chair off the floor. The wall behind him kept him and the chair from going over.

His voice was hoarse. "We're gonna need more than what Beth's got to offer."

I agreed. I plucked my phone from my back pocket and texted Malek a summary of the situation. I didn't wait for a response. The time difference meant that he might be sleeping—if gods slept. He could be working, or in Faery with Kevin, or powers only knew where. If he could help, he'd show.

The sick should be lying down, not sitting around the table. They shouldn't go to their rooms—we couldn't keep an eye on them behind that many closed doors.

"Move to the living room?" I asked.

"Ten-four," Miguel said.

Ben and Jess insisted on helping Red and me move the others— their combined magic helped them to withstand the effects of the soul sickness a little better. Ben's shield seemed to block the worst of it, and Jess's Watcher magic worked without her prompt to reweave the fabric of her body to fight off the symptoms. Addie's did the same. It was a small gift and a constant process—one that seemed to deplete Jess and Addie as much as the sickness itself. But their eyes looked clear and focused, and they could walk without listing or falling.

When we'd finished, four air mattresses outfitted with pillows and blankets housed Miguel, Addie, and the two kids. Sunday refused to lie flat, even though we'd made up one of the sofas for her. She propped herself up, knife in hand, ready for whatever trouble might come our way. She had more discipline than anyone else in the room, and greater skill with weapons. If she could manage it, she'd blind an intruder and slit their throat, and maybe ask questions later.

Beth brought her tattoo works down from her room and began to set up. We didn't have Stacy here to guide the magic as she'd done down at Snake Bite, but we did have Red to see the effects a tattoo in process would have on the soul, and that would have to do.

I reopened the wound that Addie had bound, giving more blood than was technically necessary to mix with Beth's own poisonous, magical blood. She added the combination to the ink.

She worked on the easiest surface to reach, which meant mostly wrists. She didn't need much skin, only enough to craft a recognizable infinity symbol. Red sat with her, concentrating his magical sight on her every move and every subtle shift of the soul in response to the ink.

Charlie and I stood guard over them for a time. I still wanted to go after Pestilence. I could tell from the way he held himself that he did, too. But there was no one else to keep our people safe if an attack came right now. No one except us.

Eventually, Charlie went to sit with Sunday. The murmur of their voices and the buzz of the tattoo gun became the baseline for my nerves as I paced the floor in my stocking feet. I touched base with the house spirit over and over again, measuring to what extent its strength had returned.

Eventually, it found its voice, sending a rush of images into my mind.

The moment it had allowed Gabriel to enter the house. The too-bright light piercing the edges of the basement side door. The scent of ash and blood.

The fiery footprints that Gabriel had left in the concrete floor.

The flash of magic as Gabriel resurrected Luna—no, not resurrected. He'd reconstituted her from the inside out by reversing the portion of the timestream that contained her death. Reversing time like that had caused the time predicament—the eternal now—that Pestilence seemed to be caught in.

The archangel hadn't used his power alone to perform that piece of magical wonder. He'd drawn from all available sources in the vicinity. There had been two sources.

The house spirit. And Luna's soul.

If her soul had originally burned along with her body, then reversing time had brought it back, as it had brought back her body. But rather than reinstalling it in the cage of Luna's flesh and bone, Gabriel had used part of it as fuel.

Why?

Gabriel didn't make mistakes. Everything he did had a purpose. He'd intended to make Luna vulnerable to possession.

I paused my pacing and rubbed the bridge of my nose.

The house spirit had been telling me why it had failed to note Pestilence's breach of the house, why it hadn't been able to alert us to what had happened to Luna until too late: because of Gabriel.

And why had Gabriel been in the house in the first place? Because I'd called him. Because I'd been angry. I'd wanted answers. I'd done whatever I had to do in order to get them. I hadn't considered consequences at the time. After all, why did I need to truck with such minor things as life-or-death consequences?

I carried the Angel of Death. *La Muerte* had my back. Could I be hurt? Sure. Could I be killed? I didn't think so. The Angel wouldn't allow it.

If Sunday and Miguel had agreed with me—well, they were Order operatives. We'd been bred to disregard our own safety, our own lives. If Red had gone along with us for the ride? Red's choices were his, and he was responsible for them. I was the only one responsible for what had happened here.

The buzz of the tattoo gun stopped. The snap of latex gloves announced that Beth had finished one tattoo and would be moving on the next shortly.

The low hum of Sunday's and Charlie's voices had trailed off— they'd fallen asleep, Sunday still propped up and ready to go to war, Charlie snuggled at her side. It would've been sweet if both of them weren't busy dying very slowly.

I couldn't even think about losing Sunday. I refused to follow that train of thought to the others, either.

I hunkered down to throw another log on the fire. The flames accepted it greedily, sparks flying.

I slowed my breathing, calming my nervous system. Inhale for a count of four. Exhale for a count of six. At the end of the third round, I heard a voice resonate in the depths of my heart.

Her soul is the answer.

I went still, listening with every fiber of my being.

The words came again, this time more softly.

As before, this was not the Angel's voice. This was something else altogether.

Who are you? I asked.

We are your longing, the voice said. Not *I*, but *we*.

What did that mean—my longing? What did my desire have to do with any of this?

The voice had nothing more to say. With every passing second, it felt further and further away. I might even have imagined the words it —they—had spoken, but I knew better.

Her soul was the answer. Whose soul? There was only one we'd been discussing of late. Luna's. But Luna's soul was gone.

I mulled over other possibilities as the night wore on, until Beth had completed the last of the tattoos, and all of those who'd contracted the soul sickness slept, the worry wiped from their faces in favor of a tenuous peace.

Beth slipped off her final pair of gloves, wadding them into her fist and coming to stand beside me. "Did you hear back from Malek?"

I looked at her. "How'd you know I texted him?"

"It was the logical thing to do."

Yes, but that wasn't all. "You report in to him?"

"Same as every day," she said.

"You tell him Pestilence has taken a vessel?"

She nodded. "I know he won't be happy about that. He'll probably hold you responsible."

I shrugged.

She chuckled.

"What's funny?"

"Nobody wants to be held responsible by Malek. It's almost always bloody and awful. It's nice to see someone else treat him like a person instead of the bogey man for a change."

Was that what I was doing? I didn't have it in me to get worked up about what Malek liked or disliked. "I have more important things to worry about."

"Saving people. Hunting Pestilence."

I raised a brow.

"Only certain types of TV nerds are going to get that one."

"I get it just fine," I said. "How long will the ink hold off the soul sickness?"

"Not as long as the spell Malek inked for Charlie, but pretty close."

That would have to be good enough. I would have to be good enough to get the job done. "Thank you."

"No worries." She hesitated. "Are you going to go after Pestilence—chase it through time?"

"That's one option."

"There are others?" she asked.

"Drawing it here," I said.

"I hate that one."

"Me, too."

"You should go see Red first," she said.

I glanced over my shoulder. He'd taken off. I hadn't seen or heard him go.

"He went to your room. He's fucking beat."

"Thanks for that, too," I said.

"You're going to need him to get through this. His magic. His judgment. He's going to need a few hours before he can handle whatever you're thinking about throwing at him next."

I stared at her, trying to discern an ulterior motive behind her words. Any reason other than the obvious that she would want me to hold off.

She shook her head. "There's no 'there' there. Just thinking out loud, Night. Also, these guys will be awake in a couple of hours, raring to kick somebody's ass. Except they won't have enough juice to do it."

I nodded and turned on my heel to walk away.

She reached out, laying a hand on my arm. "You know, I think what's happening between you and the Angel is exactly what's supposed to happen. I wonder if it's that way with all the other Horsemen—that they're, I don't know, bonded with their human vessels."

"Like Kevin and the Faery Queen," I said.

"Kevin is a special case, but something like that, yeah."

She let go of me and went back to cleaning up after the tattoo work.

When Kevin told me about his special case, he'd said something that had stuck with me—that we bring who we are into any such alliance. If he was right, then who he was in every facet informed not only his role as Faery King, but his merging with the Faery Queen as well. A spirit marriage, they called it.

Kevin and the former Queen might've started out as two people—or one living person and one who'd passed on—but they'd ended up as one. And that new being had as much of Kevin in him as it did the Queen.

I rubbed my eyes and stepped into Red's and my room, pushing the door closed behind me. All of the lights were off, the only illumination rising from the screen of Red's smart phone, tossed on the night table by his side of the bed.

He sat on the edge of the mattress, bent forward, resting his elbows on his knees. As my eyes adjusted to the darkness, I could see his hands curled into fists.

CHAPTER 10

I COULDN'T MAKE OUT his face, only the grass and earth of his halo and something else new—the scent of rain. I sent a spark of energy along the heart link.

He didn't send an answer. The connection between us felt hollowed out. It was as if he wasn't really there at all.

I settled beside him, bedsprings creaking under my weight. This close, I felt the heat flowing in waves from his skin. He began to glow with it, shining in the darkness like a beacon of hope—or destruction.

"Do you want to talk about it?" I asked.

His voice was gruff. "What's there to talk about?"

Maybe it'd been a mistake, following him soon. Maybe he needed some time to sit with whatever he'd seen while Beth had inked the spells on our friends.

Maybe he needed time to process the fact that people we loved would die if we couldn't find a way to save them from an incurable illness.

"Do you want me to go?"

He shook his head. "Talk to me, Night. Tell me you know what to do."

"I don't know," I said. "But I'm far from giving up."

He studied his hands. "I got a good look at what the sickness does. It's leaching the life from their souls. It takes their hope, Night. It eats their dreams. It erases everything that makes them who they are. It destroys their ability to connect with other people—with anything at all. The ink doesn't stop that from happening. It just slows it down. That's worse than death."

Every single word hit me like a punch to the gut. It stole my air. It broke my heart.

I'd thought I understood the soul sickness before in the abstract. I had a deep understanding of it in my blood and bones—how it felt to slowly kill a soul. How it felt to be soulless.

I'd never heard it described in gruesome detail before.

I'd done nothing to deserve the unlooked-for grace that had been granted me. No idea how it'd happened, or why.

It was one thing for that to happen to me. It was another thing entirely for it to happen to people I loved.

"If I hadn't summoned Gabriel—"

Red interrupted. "I was right there with you. I could've said something. I could've put the brakes on."

"No," I said. "This isn't your fault."

He turned to me. "Then whose fault is it?"

"Mine."

Saying that out loud made it real in a way that thinking it had not. I exhaled a shaky breath.

His voice built, power filling it as if it were a spell. "I think this whole situation is impossible. Even with the training you and Sunday and Miguel have—even with the Angel in our court, and the knowledge and power that Addie carries as a Watcher—it always feels like we're a step behind. Like we're going for broke. Losing is not an option. Not with the kind of stakes we're dealing with.

"How are you supposed to anticipate everything? You can't. How are you supposed to juggle the whims of an archangel or two? Mix that up with a clueless woman like Luna—no idea what she's into before it up and kills her. Add in Pestilence, who's been God knows where for God knows how long, waiting for its time to come, with the big picture agenda and its own needs and desires."

In a way, it was a spell—a litany of all the shit we'd faced in the last twenty-four hours that didn't even touch on everything that had come before. Or what might come after, if we lived to see it.

I rested a tentative hand on his leg. I needed to touch him to steady myself. To steady us both.

He looked at my hand. When he looked up again, I could see the shine of tears in his eyes. "Tell me how, Night."

"We can't," I said. "There's no way to anticipate. No rulebook or guidelines to follow. The way Michael talked about Gabriel—how Gabriel acted about what he did to Luna, the things he said to me—it's as if they believe everything that's happening now is already written."

"Fated," Red said.

"I can't believe that," I said. "If I let myself go there, then everything I've fought for means nothing."

"What if it does—what if it means nothing? What if it doesn't count for shit in the end?"

We'd had this conversation before, or some version of it. About what kind of world we wanted to build in the aftermath of the fight, provided we lived to see it. About what we were willing to do or not.

I didn't want to live in a world where my choices and my actions didn't matter.

The question was, whom they mattered to.

"Does everything we've done and said count for you?" I asked.

He stared at me, wide-eyed in the dark. After a moment, he released the fists he'd made and reached to cup my cheek in one trembling hand. "Yes."

I laid my hand over his. "It does for me, too."

"So we're fighting for ourselves," he said.

"Ourselves and other people like us—magical or not. The ones the powers are so cruel about screwing over."

He nodded. "Sometimes I think it would be better to be normal. To be blissfully unaware that any of this is happening at all. You ever feel that way?"

"At least a million times, watching them go about their everyday lives, wondering what it would be like to be able to go get a cup of coffee in the morning at a café and not have to watch my back. When I used to open the gym for the earliest class, and there would be hardly anyone on the street, I'd watch them."

"But we've never been normal," he said.

"Once upon a time, before our magic manifested."

"I don't remember much about what it was like to be five."

"Me neither."

"Do you think they're happier?"

"The normals?" I hadn't spent much time around them compared to the time I'd spent around magicians, but I understood enough to answer. "No, I don't think so. Their world is just as fucked up as ours, and they have no magic to help them cope, or to use in a fight. Some of them are sensitive enough to magic that, even if they don't have any active power, they know that something is deeply wrong with the world. With how we live in it."

He took that in. The set of his shoulders dropped a little. "We need to fix this. What happened to Faith—the god taking her over—was bad enough. I can't lose the others."

"I'm with you," I said.

"Can we track down Pestilence?" he asked. "Charlie got a bead on it?"

"That's next on my list."

"There's a list?"

"It's a short one."

"That the only item on it?" he asked.

"No," I said. "Right now, I need to make sure you get some rest. Even if it's just a power nap, Red."

He shook his head. "I don't want to sleep. I shouldn't be tired."

"But you're exhausted."

"My heart hurts, Night."

"Mine, too." I drew his hand away from my face and kissed his palm.

He lay back, curling on his side. "Stay with me?"

I tucked myself inside the curve of his body, marshaling my breath to slow the beat of my heart. I felt him struggle with sleep, not wanting to give in, but his breathing calmed eventually, deepening until sleep stole him away.

I lay awake in the dark, listening for trouble and praying for none, eyes wide open.

The house spirit seemed to have regained most of its strength, but I refused to leave it to guard us all alone. Someone should stay awake. The way things had turned out, that someone would have to be me.

Silence settled like a lead weight that made it hard to move. Hard to breathe. I could no longer hear all the little sounds that I took for granted—the patter of rain on the windows, the clacking of bare tree branches in the wind, the ticks and creaks of the house settling.

If I remained here, I'd fall asleep in spite of my best intentions. I needed to check the locks—mundane and magical. Make a cup of coffee. Think.

I slid away from Red and slipped out of the bedroom, padding down the hall into the kitchen, realizing I'd been holding my breath only after I stepped inside to find the room empty. In a house this crowded—and filled with other former operatives bent on puzzling out our situation—it was hard to find time alone.

The tick of the clock was huge in the absence of other sounds. The pots and pans that should've been sitting on the stove filled with congealing breakfast makings had been washed and stuffed into the dish drainer next to the sink. A small plate covered in plastic wrap sat on the counter, a thin sheet of notebook paper tucked beneath it.

Found this in the freezer. It's not "food" food, but it's better than nothing. Plus, chocolate. – Beth

I pulled back the plastic wrap to uncover an enormous, mostly defrosted slice of chocolate layer cake with chocolate ganache frosting.

I glanced back at the note.

P.S. There's more in the fridge for Red when he wakes up. And fresh coffee in the pot. You're welcome.

I poured a mug full of caffeine, grabbed a fork from the drawer, and set up my feast at the kitchen table, settling into the chair nearest the back door. In spite of the double-paned glass and the blinds on the windows, the outdoor chill seeped in, raising the skin on my arms to gooseflesh. At the first bite of cake, the richness of it shot the volume on all of my senses to high. It felt as if the room and everything in it had suddenly gone from black-and-white to full color.

Something tapped twice on the window. Could've been a stray branch—if there'd been any trees or bushes against the windows.

I let my magic rise and pulled the string on the blinds, which rose to half-mast with a whir, and stared straight into the black eye of a big fat crow perched on the sill.

It looked at me with unexpected intelligence and impatience. It didn't make a sound, not even a ruffling of feathers, but I heard it speak all the same. Another voice in my head, but this time, a welcome one.

You are Night.

Kevin? I asked.

It ruffled its feathers and raised its beak, seeming indignant. *Kevin sent me.*

The crow was a messenger, not a direct conduit. I'd do well to remember that.

Yes, it said, answering my thought.

What's the message? I asked.

Confirm desired location for portal in your world that will lead to the King.

A few hours ago, I'd have said the house, but now the place was filled with soul-sick people. We were vulnerable to attacks from the Order, the End, Shadow—our list of enemies continued to reveal itself.

Pestilence had run away from us and toward whatever it longed for, but I knew in my gut—and the Angel knew—that it would return.

Building a portal here would only endanger more people, human and non-human.

We needed another place we could control. One near enough to reach quickly in an emergency. A couple of places fit that bill—Ben's house being the most private, but it was a house in a neighborhood filled with people I didn't want to endanger. Been there, done that, and only because we fought Watchers who wanted to stay hidden had we skated past disaster there. And although Ben's father traveled most of the time, he did occasionally come home.

The area around the other place was lousy with people, too, but we had a little more control.

Justice Gym, I said. *You know where that is?*

Red's house.

That's not his house, I said.

The place where he takes in travelers and magicians, the crow said. *Where he creates a home for them.*

I stared at the bird. It stared back at me. It took me a second to realize that it was waiting for any further instructions or information I might have.

Tell Kevin that someone will need to come to us. We won't be able to meet him there—at least not yet.

Received. The crow cocked its head. *You bring who you already are to what you become.*

Kevin had said the same thing to me when we'd met. When we'd talked about what it meant to be transformed magically into something not human.

That part of the message from Kevin, or from you? I asked.

Take it as you will, the crow said.

Which was not an answer at all.

Thank you, I said.

The crow launched itself from the sill with a caw, fading into the rain-soaked darkness.

I set down my fork and picked up my mug, sipping coffee, letting its heat and caffeine help me to clarity.

Too much had happened that I hadn't been able to stop. I felt small, like a woman at the edge of a vast ocean with a storm raging all around, unable to hold her feet as the water rushed in. The lives of people I loved depended on my ability to reverse that incoming tide. All the worlds depended on me to find a way to stop Pestilence from wreaking havoc on magical beings first, and the humans he would decimate later as the Apocalypse picked up steam.

Then there was Luna, who I hadn't gotten time to know. Whom Gabriel had pulled into this life and death battle against her will. Who'd traveled through time and died twice and come back without a soul, prisoner to the Horseman that possessed and controlled her body.

Through it all, *La Muerte* hadn't been of any more help than I had. He had no answers to give.

He'd come through in unimaginable ways, saving my bacon—saving my everything, leading me to exactly what I needed to know. I'd expected the same again and it hadn't come to me, but I couldn't exactly be disappointed or pissed about it.

The Angel had never been human. He leaned on me for the human touch. For my knowledge of what it meant to be a fragile, embodied, flesh-and-blood being with physical needs, emotional connection, and a conscience that wouldn't allow me to rest until I satisfied it—what it meant to have a soul.

The Angel reaped souls. He sent them on to the next adventure, which I understood as many-fold. Not the traditional Heaven or Hell, necessarily, but more like a plethora of choices that an individual soul could make. A soul could reincarnate, for instance, if it still had work to do. It could travel to other worlds. Souls could evolve, too, although the nuances of that escaped me.

The souls that had joined to create the single star of beauty inside of my heart, my alchemical soul, had chosen to do just that. Maybe they'd felt I'd deserved that gift. Maybe it hadn't been about what I deserved, but instead what I needed. What the worlds needed.

In emergencies or crises, you looked around at who stood with you, their skills and personalities and drive. People helped in whatever ways they could, even if they weren't the perfect people for the job. They answered need.

So it didn't matter, really, whether I deserved the second chance I'd been given or whether I was the perfect—or even the right one—for the job.

The voice within that had spoken to me—it hadn't been *La Muerte's* voice. It wasn't my subconscious or some other part of me, nor was it the voice of anyone I recognized. Not *mi abuelita*. Not Shadow. Not Malek. The voice didn't belong to any of my crew, or to my daughter.

No stranger that I'd ever known had been able to breach my boundaries like that, not without an invitation. Unlikely that someone had found a way at this stage of the game, with my sharper edges and the Angel's all-encompassing wings acting as blade and shield against enemies. That left open the possibility that the voice belonged to one of the souls that lived within me.

I closed my eyes, turning more deeply inward, listening with every fiber of my being and searching with my inner eye for a sign that would guide the way to the answer I sought.

I drew a deep breath, concentrating on the way the air expanded my lungs, the rise of my chest and belly. The flow of blood in my arteries and veins, rich with oxygen and nutrients or heavy with the waste my cells produced, traveled from and to my heart. The thump-thump of the heart muscle itself, the movement that kept me alive, overtook my awareness.

My heart—the seat of my life. It was also the seat of my love. Of my magic. Of my soul.

I shifted my inner vision, gazing beyond the muscle and into the heart link with Red. The love that flowed through the link remained steady, regardless of whether one of us slept. Beneath the link, the deep roots of my magic, velvet black as a cloudless night sky and filled with the stars that reflected the power of all the worlds—the being that some called God. Not an old white man with a beard who presided over creation. Not separate from the worlds at all. No, God's body and spirit *were* the worlds and the universes beyond them, divinity present and immanent in all things. In all people. In all beings.

Underneath the darkness and wholeness of my magic, my patched-together soul waited, its parts not welded seamlessly together, but held together by will and choice like a nest of spotted moths clinging to each other, antennae tasting and testing the air, wings fluttering and settling over and over again. Comfortable in the dark. Drawn to the light. Holding on to connection. Ready to fly.

A single moth broke from the others, winding and circling, wings driving, its spots like eyes.

The moth felt familiar, but not like home—a part of my soul to be sure, but not one that had been a part for very long. It felt new and disoriented and grieving.

It felt like Luna.

Whom I hadn't killed. Whose soul should have moved on to its next adventure, but instead had clung to mine.

Why? I asked.

The collective spoke for her, its voice a cacophony that unsettled me. *This is where I belong.*

You think you belong with me?

With you and your Horseman.

The Angel?

Yes. Keep me safe.

There was nothing safe about the Angel of Death. Nothing safe about the situation we were in or about me—the Angel's human vessel, former assassin, tasked with stopping the Apocalypse. I didn't have room for one more soul to caretake. Other things took precedence over Luna's need for safety.

Hide me, she said.

From what?

Not what—who. Pestilence.

Was that where Pestilence had gone—to look for Luna's soul? I didn't need her to respond to know the answer. That was exactly what Pestilence had done.

The Angel spoke then. *I can send you away, Luna—far enough that the Horseman may never find you. Do you want me to do that?*

Safe with Night, she said. *Only with Night.*

Because of the Angel? I asked.

Because of you, she said.

But there was nothing special about me that could make her safe.

It's an illusion, Luna. There's no such thing as safety—not really. There's what you fear and what you love. You have to choose between them.

But I'm afraid of everything, she said.

She had every right. There was no blame or shame in that. *What do you love?*

She didn't answer. Maybe she didn't have an answer to that question.

I asked a different one. *What do you want to love?*

Charlie's face bloomed in my mind, sweat on his brow, golden hair falling into his eyes. I saw him as she'd first seen him—as a dangerous kid who'd wanted to take something from her, and then as a friend on the run. She'd wanted to help him. She'd hid him. She'd saved his life.

That vision faded, replaced by the moment she'd knocked on Addie's door, the wind whipping through the trees, the rain coming down sideways to soak her as she shivered on the porch in the darkness before dawn. I felt the hope that had filled her heart when she'd first glimpsed Addie's face, and the kindness in Addie's brown eyes.

The memories vanished.

Now, Luna began to pray, a single litany, over and over again.

I pray the Lord my soul to keep.

Words from a nightly prayer. A child's prayer. I fought the reflex to speak it with her—a remainder of my childhood, back when I'd been truly innocent, before the magic and the Order.

Who was Luna praying to, exactly? I was no god, and neither was the Angel. I couldn't save Luna's soul, and neither could he.

A muffled sound that seemed to come from outside tore me away from talk of souls and safety and gods. I wanted to block it out. I wasn't yet done talking or listening. Too many things I needed to know.

But the sound insisted. After a moment, it became less a sound than another voice. Raised, with a pronounced East Texas drawl.

My heart beat once. Twice.

I saw Red's face. Gazed into his eyes. He was with me in the depths, with all of the parts of my soul.

He'd followed the heart link down. He saw what I saw. Knew what I knew. Felt what I felt.

He spoke my name.

Night.

The word echoed inside of me.

Follow me back home, he said.

I did what he asked, up and out, finally blinking into the dim light of the kitchen, focusing my vision slowly on Red's shaggy salt-and-pepper hair, furrowed brow, and green eyes. His thick mustache. His lips moved.

"Night!"

It took some effort to make my mouth and vocal cords work in concert. "Here."

"I couldn't rouse you. Something was wrong."

I shook my head. "Just deep."

He'd slid my chair sideways from the table with me in it, and I hadn't felt a thing. He'd gone down on one knee as if he'd planned to pop the question, but held no ring. He'd wrapped his hands around my forearms, squeezing tightly enough to leave bruises.

"You can let go of me," I said.

He released the pressure, but not the hold. "Look at me."

"Thought I was."

"No."

I blinked again, forcing my eyes to focus more tightly. To feel his hands on me, and the soles of my stocking feet on the tile. To absorb the chill that seeped in past the windows and the blinds, marking the goose bumps it raised on my skin. My mug on the table still held some warmth—a bit of steam escaped into the air. I breathed in the perfume of chocolate cake and the silver glint of the fork and the shadow of the plate on the oak surface and Red's grass-and-earth.

My senses were confused. Synesthesia, they called that.

I met Red's gaze. "How long were you calling my name?"

"A good few minutes."

"You wake everyone in the whole damn house?"

"You don't think it was worth that?" he asked.

A wave of pain began at the base of my skull and rolled forward to my frontal lobe. I reached up, pressing the heel of my hand against my forehead. "Damn."

"Aspirin?"

"Whatever Addie's got," I said.

He pushed to his feet and headed for the counter, rummaging through the last cabinet to produce an industrial-size white bottle. He held it up for me to see.

Ibuprofen.

"Yeah?" he asked.

"Yeah."

He tossed it to me.

I caught it, no problem. My reflexes were on point.

He seemed to relax a little at that.

I downed three pills with the rest of the coffee while he pulled the closest chair from its spot, flipped it around, and straddled the seat.

"Where'd you go?" he asked.

"To take a look at my soul."

He raised a brow. "What'd you see?"

"The collective of souls that joined to create my whole soul. The ones that have been there from the moment my second chance began. And one brand new stray soul that has no place there, hiding—Luna's."

"What?"

"She shouldn't be there, but she is."

"Made possible by the Angel?"

"Yes." I didn't need confirmation from *la Muerte*. I knew that it was true. Every molecule in my body said so. "She won't move on. She wants me to save her."

"How in the hell are you supposed to do that?" he asked.

"I wish I knew."

He wrapped his fingers around the chair back. "The hits keep coming."

"Over my head," I said. "At the bottom of the ocean with a couple of lead weights chained to my feet."

"What can I do?"

"Look at me and tell me what you see."

"A woman with a heart that's so much bigger than she knows," he said.

I shook my head. "That's not what I meant."

"I know," he said. "You want me to use my magic to look inside? I'm not gonna see anything you don't already know is there. Your patchwork soul. Luna holding on for dear life. The Angel of Death, whatever the fuck he's doing to you. What you're really asking is for me to tell you who you are, and none of those things define you. You want me to tell you that you can handle this. That the solution will magically appear and you'll know what to do to save Luna and stop Pestilence. That you can hold off the end of the world for one more day."

I stared at him. "Yes."

"I can't do that," he said. "It's not because I don't believe in you. Christ, Night, if I didn't, I wouldn't be here. I'd have run far away at the first out you gave me. I believe in you, and I love you, and you are not a god."

The same thought I'd had a moment ago, before he'd interrupted my inward-seeing. My eyes filled. I blinked back hot tears, refusing to let them fall.

"What do you want to do?" he asked.

In this moment, I wanted to be anywhere but here. Find a quiet desert island or mountaintop and set myself up off the grid, where I could pretend that none of this was happening. Where I could catch my breath and make room to think and come up with some kind of answer that made sense to my head and my heart.

But that would never happen. I couldn't let go. I couldn't turn away.

Fighting was my only option.

This battle didn't look like any I'd fought before. It smelled different. It tasted different. I couldn't kill Pestilence. I couldn't win a battle of will against it, either—not one that would stick, anyway. The Angel and I might be stronger, but a being as powerful as Pestilence would find a way around any binding we used.

If I couldn't kill or bind, I'd have to negotiate. I needed leverage.

What did I have that could break—or bend—Pestilence?

"I need to find the Horseman," I said.

"You'll need Charlie, then."

"Yes. I wish we had Miguel for backup, just in case."

"Better if he and the others stay here and keep still. They'd only make themselves worse off if they went with you, and they're not at full strength, so any help they might want to give could come off half-baked."

"I know," I said. "The only difference between them and Charlie is that the magic holding off his death is stronger. Using his power will only add fuel to the fire of what's killing him."

"It didn't stop him before from traveling back for Luna."

"Nothing could've stopped him."

"Remind you of anyone?" Red asked.

I ignored that. In the dictionary, under *stubborn*, Red could find entries for every single person in this house, himself included. We all wanted to do the right thing. Not a coward among us in that regard, no matter the price.

Luna was the only one who'd admitted running in the face of danger as standard operating procedure. She wanted to be safe. She stayed with me because she thought I would keep her safe.

I tapped my fingers on my thigh.

"What are you thinking, Night?"

I didn't want to say it out loud, because the sound of my voice would make it real.

I might already be the monster Michael warned me I could become.

CHAPTER 11

CHARLIE FURROWED HIS BROW so deeply, it all but disappeared, leaving a cap of gold hair and eyes filled with an alchemy of confusion and worry. He tucked his thumbs beneath his suspenders, tugging at the elastic. He looked impossibly young, sitting at the kitchen table in front of a plate of whole wheat peanut butter toast I'd placed in front of him. Three slices.

"I can feel the Horseman," he said. "And I can take you to it, but I can't tell you when he is."

Red settled in the seat next to Charlie, having added half a jar of grape jam to his otherwise identical breakfast and smashed the whole thing into a triple-decker PB&J. "Sounds like a contradiction in terms."

"Not at all," Charlie said. "The time Pestilence has gone to is… before we reckoned such a thing as time at all."

I slid two more slices of bread into the toaster oven and turned the dial. The heating elements began to glow orange. The coffee maker burbled, halfway to full pot status. Outside, night gave up the ghost, the darkness making way for light.

"Before time?" Red asked. "We talking dinosaurs here?"

"Before."

"The world is a molten ball of lava?"

"It hasn't yet come into being," Charlie said. "As if God said 'Let there be light,' but light has not yet been born. The breath before creation."

"That's—" Red blinked. "I don't know what that is."

I turned toward them and leaned back against the counter. "Let's go with weird. What's at the beginning of all things that a Horseman could want?"

"A heart-to-heart with Daddy?" Red bit into his sandwich.

"Possible," I said.

"But?"

"But it doesn't track," I said. "If there is a capital-G God, and he's still around here somewhere, Pestilence wouldn't have had to travel all the way back in time to the moment the worlds were born to talk with him."

"Then what?" Red asked.

"Pestilence is bitter," I said. "Hurt."

"You're shitting me."

"I saw it in the Horseman's mind."

"What does a being that powerful have to be bitter and hurt about?" Red asked. "Or better yet, answer me this—assuming that there's a good reason for it to feel that way—what makes Pestilence different from the rest of us miserable bastards?"

Charlie cocked his head. "You're miserable?"

Red set down his sandwich, then folded his arms across his chest. "It's a rhetorical question."

No, it wasn't. Not entirely. I'd been in the bedroom with him when his steadiness faltered. I'd seen the way what had happened since the Angel appeared on our doorstep—since *I'd* appeared on his doorstep—tore him to shreds inside. I wished that could be different. I didn't know how to change it. The only way out of the Apocalypse was to stop it from happening. The only way out of that was through.

I swallowed hard. "First, immortality. It's one thing to go a human lifespan with this stuff, and something else to deal with it for eternity."

Red stared at me, unmoved.

"Second, it was created to do harm. To kill. Maybe it exists in the service of life—to perpetuate all the worlds, to keep all of life from extinguishing—but, even if that were true, what would it be like to live an eternal life where everything you touch rots and dies?"

That earned me narrowed eyes. "You almost sound as if you feel sorry for Pestilence."

"I don't think I understand," Charlie said.

"Pestilence was created to kill. It has no other purpose. Who the hell knows how long it's been wandering around the worlds in spirit form, but the call has come for it to possess a human body and get to work in earnest. Which means more harm. More killing. And no choice but to do what God or whoever made it to do."

"If it were me," Red said, "I'd want it to end. All of it. The only way to make my suffering end would be to do my job to the best of my ability."

I nodded. "But it's not out there doing that."

A thought bloomed in my mind the second the words rolled off my tongue. I pushed away from the counter.

"What?" Red asked.

"It's possible that Pestilence is pulling a run-and-hide. Go back to the beginning, before all of the killing, where it could just be."

"Presuming that it has a heart and a conscience," Charlie said.

Red glanced at him. "Big assumption. What's the second choice? I can see it written all over your face, Night."

"That it's gone back to the beginning for the opposite reason."

"To kill the worlds before life has a chance," Red said.

"Yes," I said.

"Can it do that?"

It didn't seem plausible, but then, none of us could've predicted what had gone down since the Angel had appeared. "I don't know. But if that's Pestilence's plan, we've got to stop it."

Charlie shook his head. "With one assassin, one time traveler, and one—what are you, Red?"

"I'm the one that sees what's inside a person—and calls bullshit. Sunday is down for the count. Miguel, too. We have no real access to the Watchers' magic, or even to Ben's shield. Beth is mighty in a pinch, but one of us has to stay here and guard our people, preferably someone with enough juice to turn back an attack. That's her. So unless you're planning to call in reinforcements from Texas, Charlie's right. We're on our own. We can't handle this between the three of us."

"Four." We would need the Angel's magic. His power.

"Okay, four. My point still stands. You talked earlier about leverage. If Pestilence is planning to end us all before we even get started, and it's committed to doing that, there's no leverage in the universe that will hold it back."

I shook my head. "I don't believe that's true."

"But you can't be sure."

"I can't be sure of anything," I said. "It doesn't matter. We have to act."

Charlie took a deep breath and blew it out slowly. "I agree."

Red looked from Charlie to me. "Never give up?"

I nodded.

"Even if it gets you killed. Even if when it's all said and done, you're utterly changed."

There it was. He'd said he trusted me. Believed in me. That, even if the Angel and I merged into one being or I became the Angel of Death, I would still be me. He'd believed every word he'd spoken. But, as he'd said, we couldn't be sure how things would turn out.

Charlie stood, avoiding looking either of us in the eye. "I'm going wake Sunday—if I can wake her. I'll tell her what we're planning. She'll have some comments."

"I bet she will," Red said.

We watched Charlie walk out of the kitchen, holding silence until his footfalls faded.

"Everything we've faced so far has changed us," I said.

"I can't disagree," he said. "If we're putting our cards on the table here, I have to tell you that I'm worried. That I'm scared."

I met his gaze. "I don't want to lose you, either."

"I know." He reached for me through the heart link, the magical pulse strong and unwavering.

Cards on the table.

I reached back. I didn't try to shield a single feeling. I let him see it all. My own worry and fear. My hope, dimmer than it once had been, but still alive.

I walked over to him, meaning to hunker down in front of him, but he drew me into his lap instead. He felt as solid as he always had, fear or no fear.

"Whatever we're about to do, I need to know that we're coming back," he said.

We both knew I couldn't promise that. "I'll do everything I can."

"That's not what I mean," he said. "I'm talking about the Angel. About how, every time you've combined your most powerful magic with his, you come away changed. Big changes."

I waited while he searched for the right words.

"If Beth is right and you do become the Angel—whatever that looks like, whatever it means—I want you to come back. You understand what I'm saying?"

Even if I bore no resemblance to myself? Even if no part of me remained human? Even if I was cold as the grave, like the Angel?

Red couldn't read my thoughts, but he could feel what I felt enough to tell what was on my mind.

"Even if your worst fears become true," he said.

If push came to shove, I had only one other place to go—to Faith. If I had to leave home, she would take me in, regardless of whether the god she carried approved. I trusted that, and I felt grateful for it. But I didn't want to leave home. To leave Red. I wanted to be with him.

The keen awareness that we didn't always get what we wanted veiled my desire like a shroud.

"Night?"

I met his gaze, the green of his eyes dark, like evergreens after a hard rain. He studied my face. The link between us thrummed. For a heartbeat, there was no one else in the whole world except the two of us.

"Yes," I said. "Now, you promise."

"Cross my heart."

He pulled me close, brushing his lips across mine. I kissed him back, relishing the taste of him, breathing him in.

"Sealed with a kiss," I said.

His lips curved. "So what's the plan?"

"You may not like it."

"All kinds of things I don't like."

I studied him. "It depends on Luna."

He cocked his head. "What do you want her to do?"

"My experience with the Angel may not be how these things usually go—listen to me, as if there's anything *usual* about this. He's taken me over more than once, but he also works with me. It's my humanity that he's curious about, that he doesn't want to lose. He doesn't understand what it's like to be human and he needs my perspective in order to do right by us and our world—all the worlds. All of that—it resides in my soul."

I hesitated.

Red waited.

"Pestilence occupies Luna's body. He's one-hundred-percent in charge."

Red's eyebrows climbed to his hairline. "The one thing he's missing in there is Luna's humanity. Because her soul isn't in her body."

I nodded.

"You want Luna to go back in there. Establish a foothold and what—tame the Horseman?"

"Something like that," I said. "There's only a couple of problems with this plan."

"Yeah," Red said. "Starting with this one: you can't ask Luna to do that."

"That's actually not a problem," I said.

"Please tell me you're joking."

I shook my head. "I can ask. It's no more than I would ask of myself."

"Luna is not you. She's a civilian, Night. She didn't even know about magic until Gabriel pulled her into this mess. You're a highly trained—"

I filled in the blank. "Killer."

"Order operative," he said. "You're used to doing what has to be done no matter the cost, which didn't turn out that great for you, in case you've forgotten."

No, I hadn't forgotten. I narrowed my eyes.

"I'm not wrong," he said.

"No."

"You can't expect her to say yes, Night."

"I don't," I said.

"So what, then—you're gonna force her?"

"I don't want to do that," I said.

"But you could."

I shrugged. "I haven't worked out what I can do and what I can't where souls are concerned. I've only just figured out that I can carry the souls of the dead with me. Or that we can. Maybe we can force her out of her hiding place and shove her soul back into her body. I don't know what would happen beyond that. She's terrified. She would have to choose something besides fear. I don't know whether she can. Hell, if I were in her shoes, I don't know whether I'd be able to."

He swallowed hard. "What's Option B?"

"No fancy logistics. The Angel and I confront Pestilence. We talk. We see where things lead. Or we fight."

"But you can't take out the Horseman."

"Maybe this time it's not about taking out the enemy."

"It's always about that," he said. "That, or buying time to get our shit together."

I closed my eyes, searching for an answer that made sense, but found none. I'd always known what to do when things came down to the wire, but now that knowledge—strategy and sacrifice, everything I'd learned in my time with the Order—had deserted me. So much for my vaunted training. So much for doing what had to be done.

"What?" he asked.

I wanted to say something smart. Something to cover over the uncertainty, and the fluttering fear that rose along with it. But I didn't want to hide. Not from Red. Not now, and not ever.

"I'm lost," I said.

"I'll find you." He wrapped his arms around me and pulled me tight, his breath warm against my cheek.

Pestilence was lost, too. It didn't have anyone—no Red, no Sunday—no one except its fellow Horsemen. It longed for something. Maybe it wanted to end it all, as Red had guessed. Or maybe it wanted some kind of connection.

That longing was the key. It had to be.

I sensed movement in the doorway a split second before Charlie cleared his throat.

"Sorry to interrupt," he said. "Sunday wants to see you, Night. And she's upstairs."

How had she managed to climb the stairs in her condition? And why?

I squeezed Red, then let him go reluctantly and met Charlie's gaze. "She say anything else?"

"You're an idiot and if she could stand upright for a minute more, she'd kick your ass?"

I rolled my eyes and stood up slowly. All of my earth-bound, embodied, outward-looking bearings had returned.

"Are you all right?" Charlie asked.

"That's not the word I'd use." I glanced over my shoulder at Red. "You want to come with?"

He shook his head. "I'm gonna pick Charlie's brain on the subject of time travel."

Charlie leaned against the doorjamb. "You are?"

"In detail," Red said.

I left them to it, heading for the stairs. My footfalls seemed preter-naturally loud on the hardwood floor. A house full of people should not be so quiet, so still. I heard only my own steps on the staircase, only the sound of my own breath in the carpeted hall, until I opened the door to Sunday's room and the hinges protested.

Sunday had propped herself up, fully clothed, on top of the

bedspread, half-sitting and half-lying down. She'd folded her hands across her belly, watching them rise and fall with her breathing. She glanced at me as I stepped in and snicked the door shut behind me.

I kept my voice pitched low. The bedrooms weren't soundproof, and people were sick and sleeping, and this might be a conversation we didn't want overheard in any case.

"So I'm an idiot?"

Sunday sighed. "You're something, all right. Are you really planning to travel through time to get to Pestilence?"

I nodded. "How's that different from going back for Luna?"

"It's not," she said. "Except in all the ways that it is. Charlie told me when the Horseman has gone to. That's big shit, Night. Have you asked Charlie about the effect it might have on your magic, going back that far?"

I shook my head. "Haven't even thought about it."

"See? That's why you need me. Why you shouldn't be going without me. Why I'm so infernally fucking pissed that I won't have your back this time."

I sat on the side of the bed. "You've got my back right now."

"It's not the same," she said. "If there's a fight, you'll be on your own."

"I've fought a lot of battles on my own, Sunday."

"You know what I mean."

I met her gaze. "I know."

She held out a hand. I took it, weaving my fingers with hers.

"You're in trouble," she said.

I didn't want to lie or hide from her, either. "I'm gonna have to play it by ear."

"You're taking Red?"

I shook my head.

"Not sure you understood that," she said. "You. Are. Taking. Red."

"He can't fight," I said.

"He does the other things super well. You're going to need that. Don't ask me how I know. I just know. Gut feeling."

"Heartburn?" I asked. That had been one of our inside jokes during our time in the Order.

She didn't laugh.

"Okay," I said.

"You're giving in that easily?"

"It could be your dying wish." She was, after all, slowly dying.

Her mouth curved. "Fuck you, Sanchez."

I lifted her hand and planted a kiss on her knuckles. "I respect your gut."

"You'd better," she said. "You do what you have to do, Night. I don't care if it's shitty. I don't care if your pre-Apocalypse self would be ashamed. You survive. You live to fight another day. You get your ass back here. You got that?"

I raised a brow. "You did not bring me up here for a pep talk."

"That's not pep talking. That's an order."

"What gives, Sunday? Why are you up here in the first place? Why expend the energy?"

She chewed her lip. "There's one more thing. Something Addie and I cooked up—well, mostly Addie. She's the one with the Watcher mojo."

"She's just as sick as you are."

"Probably sicker by now, but hopefully it'll be worth it."

I stared at her. "What did you do?"

She looked past me to the door. "Any minute now."

"What?" I demanded.

A knock sounded, loud and unexpected enough to make me flinch.

Sunday raised her voice. "Come."

Addie poked her head through the opening. Some of her color had returned—no, it only seemed that way. Her face glowed from exertion and magic, not health. Her brown eyes behind the lenses of her silver-rimmed glasses had lost all of their shine, and the bags beneath them had deepened. She held onto the door handle as if she thought she'd fall over without using it a brace.

I released Sunday's hand and rushed toward her, catching her by the forearms as she let go. "Whoa, Addie."

Even her voice sounded frail. "That's the word."

The hallway behind her was bright enough to make me squint as I glanced past her. So bright, it looked as if it were ablaze.

I smelled no smoke, but the hallway appeared to be on fire.

"The hell is that?" I asked.

"That asshole you and Sunday talk about," she said.

I knew exactly whom she meant—and that she would never call him that herself. "There's an archangel in the hall?"

"He'd be in this room if you'll move us out of the way," she said.

I did as she asked, maneuvering her toward the bed, where Sunday made room for her. Then I turned and placed myself between the people I loved and Michael.

He walked into the room as I'd seen him previously—hair, a writhing wreath of orange, yellow, red, and blue flame. Three eyes. Glittering golden armor and a sword with a golden hilt sheathed on his back.

Then, in a flash, he shifted from archangel to someone trying to masquerade as a regular guy with a heavy metal habit. Black T-shirt. Black denim jacket and faded jeans. Short, thick, black hair. The air that bent visibly around his body gave lie to the disguise—as did his pupil-less eyes, the color of the sun and filled with as much fire.

He met my gaze without blinking.

"Did he come on his own, or did you ask him to come, Addie?" I asked.

"We asked, Sunday and me. And you should speak to him directly. It's disrespectful to talk about him as if he's not here."

I glanced back to show her side-eye. We could go all day about disrespectful behavior between the two of us before we ever got to the archangel in the room.

Michael spoke, his voice cutting the air like the golden sword I could no longer see. "I won't hurt them. There's no need to protect them."

I refused to move, and I refused to relax. This wasn't just another magical being like Sunday or Red or my kid or even Malek the serpent. Michael was something else altogether. I'd bet he could barely lift a finger and still manage to alter entire worlds.

"You might not mean to hurt them," I said. "But you could, like Gabriel dosing unsuspecting people with magic."

"He doesn't mean to cause harm," Michael said.

"But he does."

He nodded, giving me the point. "Addie and Sunday have told me what you're attempting to do. I warned you that it wouldn't work."

"So you did."

"How am I to offer advice when you don't listen?" he asked.

I blinked at him. "You're here to give me shit?"

He laughed. It sounded like a firestorm, and it sent a blast wave of heat across the room—nothing hot enough, thankfully, to catch anything on actual fire.

"I'm not here to scold you," he said. "I'm here to offer help—if you're willing to take it."

I waited.

"I'm here to take Luna's soul off of your hands."

I didn't know what I'd expected to hear, but it sure wasn't that. "Sorry. What?"

"The soul of the woman, Luna. It burdens you."

That was one way to look at it. "She clings to the Angel and me."

"She clings to you."

"Because she feels safe," I said.

He closed the door and leaned back into it. "She's not safe, is she?"

He knew my thoughts—no idea how. Did it matter? He was an archangel, and his blood ran in my veins. He probably knew everything there was to know about me, more than I remembered myself.

"She's free to say no," I said.

"Is that true? That might be your intention, but I doubt that it's the Angel's intention. He will do whatever is most expedient, and he can. He can put her soul back into her body without her consent."

I shook my head. "He hasn't said as much to me."

"He shares his plans with you, then? All of them?"

I curled my hands into fists. *La Muerte* didn't tell me everything.

He told me what he thought I needed to know. Did he have plans for Luna that he hadn't shared with me? It was possible, even probable.

Michael studied my face. "I see you've reached my conclusion. Give her to me."

I may have reasoned my way to his position, but that didn't mean I would do what he asked. "What are you planning to do with her?"

"Make her unreachable," he said.

The Angel had made the same offer. He'd wanted to protect Luna from Pestilence, if that was what Luna wanted. Michael's offer smelled different. No talk of heaven. No talk of protecting her soul.

"Unreachable for whom?" I asked.

"You, of course," he said. "And the Horseman, Pestilence."

"Why would Pestilence come for her himself?"

"It will need her in order to be effective," Michael said. "It's the same with you and the Angel of Death, is it not?"

All the Angel's talk of needing my humanity, of how important it was. When he talked of needing me whole and having agency in order to do our work—to fight in service of life—I'd always assumed he meant what he said at face value.

"It is," I said.

"Without her, Pestilence is hobbled. With the power of her soul, however, the Horseman can fulfill its destiny."

"What do you mean, 'with the power of her soul'?"

"Pestilence will burn through it, slowly but surely. Use it as a power source."

I sucked in a breath. My thoughts ricocheted to the Horseman I carried.

What about *La Muerte?* Was he using my soul as fuel? Would he burn through it? Had he been lying to me, or holding back, all this time?

I looked at Michael. I saw him differently than I had even a second ago. I wanted to trust him. He'd been helpful to me, even if he gave assistance on his own terms. And he was a goddamn archangel. That should count for something. It should matter.

But telling me this—at the time and place he'd chosen to do so—

stank to high heaven. Telling me now, when he needed me to back off and let him take charge, undermining my relationship with the Angel I carried at a moment when the stakes had never been higher—when they would only get higher—would make me ineffective. I'd spend my time spinning stories about what was really going on, trying to figure out the Angel's true motive. I'd be useless while the world burned.

Why would he want that?

Michael pushed off from the door, pacing halfway to me. "The next time I warn you that what you want to do will not work—when I tell you it's impossible—will you listen, Night?"

He wanted me to believe that it had all been for nothing. Going back for Luna. Trying to save her. Calling Gabriel. Even the spell that Beth had tattooed to slow down the sickness Pestilence had dropped on nearly everyone I loved.

My magic rose within me on a tide of rage.

"Stay your hand," Michael said.

As if anything I could possibly do would hurt him. We both knew he'd wipe the floor with me in seconds. I wasn't powerful enough to touch him.

Not yet, the Angel whispered.

There it was. A reason, if not *the* reason.

"You know better than I do," I said. "That's what you're telling me."

"There are forces larger than yours—than the Angel's—in play here. You need to trust us. Otherwise, we're working at cross-purposes when we should be working together."

I could choose to believe him. He certainly seemed to believe every word that spilled from his mouth, and I heard no lie in it. He was supposed to be God's right hand. He was supposed to be the end-all, be-all of generals.

He wanted me to accept that. Okay. But he wasn't asking me to add anything to the mix. He wasn't asking the Angel, either. What he wanted was that we close the book on our free will and judgment, and allow the forces of fate to take over and run the show. He wanted us to take orders. He didn't want to be questioned.

Michael was playing the long game. He could see moving parts and patterns that I couldn't even fathom. To Michael, the big picture was all that mattered. To him, but not to me.

"What are you after?" I asked. "Not with today's proposal, but the whole thing."

Flames kindled in his eyes. "What are you asking?"

"Whose side are you on?"

"The side of life," he said.

"And your way is the only way." Not a question, but a statement.

He nodded.

"If I can't get with that program?"

"Then you'll continue to fail," he said.

I said nothing. There was nothing left to say.

"Will you give Luna to me?" he asked.

The Angel's wings fluttered near my heart and, along with them, the smaller, more delicate wings that belonged to her soul. The voice I'd come to think of as that of the dead who'd formed my own soul uttered a single word.

It rose through my heart and throat, into my mouth. It tasted of steel and blood, of magic and marshaled will. I spoke it with my own voice, answering for us all.

"No."

The sound of it reverberated within me, in the marrow of my bones and through the current of my blood. It echoed through the room and beyond, into the house.

Michael heard the power in it. He held my gaze, his fire to my darkness.

One moment, our eyes locked. The next, he'd gone—vanished without a trace. Unlike Gabriel, he hadn't left footprints burned into the floor. The asshole had some manners.

Addie's voice was hard. "Night?"

I turned to look at her and saw the same anger in her eyes that I knew simmered in mine.

Addie felt a deference toward angels that I didn't, but that was in her nature, in her magic. She was a Watcher. Descended from fallen angels, her whole life beholden to the Angel I carried within me.

"You did right," she said.

"Did I? You summoned Michael with the best of intentions, and I just told him to fuck off in so many words."

"If I'd known what he would say…."

"You didn't."

She pressed her lips into a thin line. "They can't be allowed to control what happens from here. They don't know everything even if they pretend to. They don't know what it's like to be human, for one. Or fae. Or, when it comes down to it, demon. They'll fight to the best of their ability, and, with them at the helm, we might come out on top. But what kind of world will there be afterwards?"

I loosened my fists, belatedly realizing I'd punched half-moons into my palms. "I never got that far."

"That's all right," she said. "Is it true what he said—that you carry Luna's soul now as well?"

I nodded.

"Did she want to go with him?"

No, in spite of the fact that she had to know by now that I wanted her to do the unthinkable. The thing she feared more than anything in all the worlds. Staying with me was preferable to being made unreachable, which to me sounded like a euphemism for having her soul murdered once and for all, with no hope of whatever heaven or grace or peace might be possible.

I shook my head.

Luna wanted that grace. That peace. She wanted what was hers. What belonged to her. Her birthright.

"It would've been a betrayal for you to give her to him," Addie said.

"Night wouldn't do that," Sunday said. "Would you?"

Sunday pushed herself further upright. Even that little movement seemed to exhaust her. She met my gaze, her blue eyes daring me to live up to the person she knew me to be.

Everyone seemed so sure about what I would or wouldn't do. Where I would succeed and where I would fail.

Everyone except me.

CHAPTER 12

T HE BASEMENT'S CHILL seeped through my clothes and through my skin, diving directly for my bones. The circle in the center of the protections—rugs, pillows, ghosts of the dead—waited for us with bated breath. Gabriel's burnt footprints pointed the way.

The quiet down here, like the silence in the house, was a constant reminder that the people we loved were down for the count, maybe forever. Charlie himself served as a reminder of the magical sickness that would kill them all if we failed.

We would have no help from them other than what they'd already given. We would have no help from Michael or Gabriel. We had only each other. Only ourselves.

Beth would stay behind to guard. She'd set up in the kitchen, her magic twined with the house spirit's, watching and waiting. I'd found her at the table as morning faded into afternoon, the patter of rain on the windows an irritating constant, the sky gray with clouds and late December gloom. She hadn't drunk much of the coffee cooling in her mug.

She'd looked at me briefly when I'd walked in, her gaze darting to Ben and Jess, her companions at the table.

Jess wore purple pajamas covered with angry white kitties, their *meows* imprisoned in cartoon speech bubbles. The normal glow of her brown skin was subdued. Even the big gold hoops in her ears seemed to have lost their shine. She'd taken the pins from her hair, her curls untamed. Her starry Watcher's halo sparkled, but sluggishly.

Ben's white T-shirt and holey jeans had seen a few too many washes. His white skin had gone so pale, it looked almost translucent. His long brown hair hung in his eyes. He fingered the soul patch on his chin with one hand, and with his other held onto Jess.

His gray halo still looked solid, his ability to shield both Jess and himself from the worst effects of the sickness still on point.

They'd come to sit with Beth because they couldn't stand to lie in bed any longer, waiting to die. They might not have access to their full magical strength, but they'd lend what they could to Beth in the event something went wrong.

They just wanted to help. To do *something*.

I knew how they felt.

Looking at them hurt my heart. It raised a fear that wanted to run rampant through me. Nothing could happen to them. Nothing. I refused to allow it.

I tried to show them that. They saw. They knew.

Beth set down her mug, finally meeting my gaze. "Whatever you have to do, Night."

"I promise," I said.

Jess raised her chin. "Make us proud."

I'd shown her a wry grin, and it'd taken everything in my power to keep my mouth from trembling. I hadn't felt proud. I'd felt like an imposter. A snake in the grass. A monster masquerading as a woman.

Whatever I had to do, it could not be good. I couldn't see any way to end this that didn't involve blood or terror.

The three of them still sat in the kitchen. There, they would remain until we returned. I felt their presence above us. I trusted the three of them. I wanted to be worthy of their trust, too.

Jess's words echoed in my head.

If I couldn't put my faith in the archangels, I would place it in my lover and my friends. My family. Compared to the powers, we were small, but we were not insignificant.

I breathed in the chill and blew it out slowly. The basement protections held us secure. I gave thanks to the house spirit for its work. I gave thanks to the house itself for shelter and home.

I met Red's gaze. I remembered my oaths to him, and he remembered his to me. I breathed in his grass and earth and hoped it wouldn't be the last time. He was about to walk into the unknown with me.

Sunday's insistence had made an impression on me. She wanted him to watch my back in her stead, sure—but, more than that, I had a feeling that I would need Red's magic. That I'd never be able to turn the tide without him.

There was just one problem. Where we were headed, there wouldn't be any air to breathe. No atmosphere at all. No gravity. Nothing to hold onto except each other. Where we were going, it would be impossible for humans to survive, and Red was, at the root of all things, human.

Fear of what might happen to him wanted to take root in my belly. I kept it at bay with great effort.

"You stay with me," I said. "You hold on and don't let go. You understand?"

He nodded. "We've got the heart link," he said. "I won't let go."

The Angel would keep me alive and whole, and through the heart link, I would extend that magic to Red. But we couldn't know how things would roll. What chance might throw our way. What unexpected things might turn our plans upside down.

"Stop worrying about my safety," he said. "Even if I stayed here, there'd be no guarantees. At least we'll be together."

That was that.

He walked over to the place Charlie had prepared for him in the circle and sat. After a moment, I followed, and settled beside him. Charlie came last, his magic flowing from his pores. The air around him wavered, as if he could step sideways at any second and flash through time.

Charlie was the door that would take Red and me to the Horseman. Charlie wouldn't be able to go all the way through with us. His soul-sickness wouldn't allow it.

We took each others' hands.

"Close your eyes," Charlie said. "I've got the rest."

I steeled myself, tasting the metallic tang of anticipation and fear that warred inside of me. I let myself feel it all—the shaky rise and fall of my breath, the flow of my magic, the feel of my weight on the floor —and then let it go.

My stomach shot into my throat. The floor vanished. We fell into the timestream.

Bodies spinning forward, slowly at first and then gaining speed to knife through the air. The stench of sulfur made me choke. Heat seared the edges of my skin. I held my breath against the burning until it passed, sucking in whatever passed for air as we moved beyond the In-Between—the gateway to all other worlds, including the world of time.

It stretched before us like a starry night, warm enough at first, but cooling as we traveled further. I tightened my grip on Red's and Charlie's hands. I didn't want to lose them. I needed them to be safe. To be whole and well.

Cool became cold, and the first shiver rocked me—it could only have been worse for them. I'd lived through much worse a handful of days ago when we'd confronted the End. The ice had frozen me solid. If it hadn't been for the Angel, I'd never have walked out of there.

His wings—my wings—fluttered near my heart.

The stars that stretched out before us became fewer and farther between. The first icicles formed on my skin. Breathing grew harder, as if I couldn't get enough air.

Charlie let go. Without his mass to hold our spinning steady, Red and I gathered still more speed, rocketing faster and faster, until I could no longer hold my eyes open. I lost all sense of my physical place in the space of the timestream. The stars grayed out, fuzzing and snowing like a channel I could no longer receive clearly. I came a hairsbreadth from passing out completely, but I held onto Red's hand —I held onto my heart, the seat of my magic, the seat of my love, the home of the heart link—as if nothing else mattered.

Red's grip felt strong. Sure. If he'd brought his fears and doubts with him, I could no longer feel them. I felt only the core of him. His heart. His love. An endless well of fierce compassion that emerged from his depths.

I've got you, the Angel said. *The Horseman is near.*

The Angel's magic flowed, the ice of the grave filling me to over-flowing. I no longer needed breath or warmth. I could do without the stuff of life—not forever, but for long enough.

Red could not. I sent a portion of the Angel's magic through the heart link. Enough to sustain him. To keep him alive and conscious and present. To protect him.

The rhythm of his heartbeat filled me. The flow of the blood in his veins. *La Muerte's* ice slowed the life inside of him, as it did for me.

The spinning slowed to a stop. Our feet settled on rock so hot, it could only be called lava. The stuff we'd landed on burned through the soles of our shoes, but didn't touch our flesh. There was nothing else, only the fire.

I caught sight of Pestilence. The Horseman had been immersed in the flow of lava. It rose from the fire, edges separating from the molten rock, burning and yet not consuming its body, which was Luna's body—like something from a nightmare.

My magic responded, my darkness twined with the Angel's dark-ness, cold fire flickering along my skin and the nubs of my wings. I felt the rise of Red's power, encased within the Angel's ice.

I placed myself between the Horseman and the man I loved, tearing my attention away from the heart link—trusting Red and trusting the Angel to hold fast.

"I've been waiting for you and your Angel," Pestilence said.

"You knew we'd come," I said. "You have my dying family as your leverage."

"I shouldn't need leverage at all. You should take your rightful place at my side. We have work to do. We have worlds to destroy, Night Sanchez."

"You talked before about fate," I said. "That you'd come because this is our time."

"It's all fate. It's all written. We should do what we're made to do. That's the only peace we'll ever have."

"Peace through oblivion?"

"Peace through destruction," it said.

"If I told you there's another way?"

"I'd say you're a liar. And I'd ask why you're speaking to me. Why my brother has not taken you over and shunted away your conscious-ness and your will. Surely he can overcome you. You're only human."

Only human. As if humanity were something Pestilence dragged in on the bottom of its shoe. As if we counted for less than nothing. As if any of us would stand back and allow it free rein without a fight.

"*La Muerte* can take over any time he wishes," I said. "He chooses not to."

The Horseman cocked its head. "Why would he make such a choice?"

There—at the close of his question—the feeling I'd sensed in its memories. Longing.

For what? For whom?

"He rebels against his purpose," I said. "Against the reason he was made. He likes this world. He's come down on the side of life."

Pestilence stared at me. "But his promise—his oath."

"Broken," I said.

What had the Angel called it? A wicked vow. A promise that should never have been made. The Angel understood that after millennia of experience. Millennia, walking the earth among the living, like a moth drawn to a flame. Among us, but never one of us. Not until now. Not until me.

"Oath breaker," Pestilence said.

"Do you want to know why?" I asked. "We can show you."

"What—how to be human?"

I nodded.

"What if I don't want to know?" Pestilence smiled. The gesture made my skin crawl. "Do you embrace your humanity, or do you run from it? It's written all over you, this battle. Love versus fear. The struggle to do what must be done, even if it makes you the monster you once were. I see it in you."

How? How could it see?

It was a Horseman, like *la Muerte.* It was an Elder power. It would always know things about me that I preferred remain hidden. But it didn't know everything.

"I will make you into that which you fear most," it said.

I shook my head. "It's my choice."

"There is no choice."

I opened my mouth to answer, but snapped it shut in the face of the rage in its eyes. The hate that roared through its black-and-green mirrored halo. The intake of breath before the Horseman's scream ripped through the time before time.

The space around us seemed to tear. Mirrored darkness the color of Pestilence's halo shredded stars. Shredded fire.

It captured my attention. Held me in thrall. It distracted in the split-second hush before Pestilence launched itself at me.

I hoped like hell that Red moved out of the way fast enough. Because I couldn't brace myself against Pestilence—it would knock me flat on my back. Steal what breath remained in my lungs. Pin me down.

I rolled backwards as Pestilence hit me, throwing the Horseman into the space behind me. Momentum carried me to a crouch again. I spun to face the Horseman. Pierced it with my gaze while I searched for Red from the corner of my eye.

Red was gone. I couldn't see him. No form. No light. No shadow.

I felt him through the heart link, but far away. I had to find him. I had to—

Pestilence ran at me again. I turned a hair before it struck. It stumbled, tripping over its feet, flame dripping from its skin.

Before it could catch its balance, I dove, taking it down from behind. It fought to turn over as I drove it into the molten rock. It screamed again, every ounce of muscle working, rolling onto its back as its head went under.

The Horseman shot out a hand, wrapping fiery fingers around my neck. I couldn't shake its iron grip.

Its face emerged from the lava, raw will shining in its eyes, teeth bared.

The place where its hand met the delicate skin of my neck burned —heat searing through the Angel's ice. A wave of nausea poured through me. A finger of dark fire touched my heart. Pestilence's greatest weapon, inside my defenses for the briefest second.

Soul sickness exploded within me in a rain of sparks.

The Angel's magic rolled over them one by one, extinguishing their fire. There were so many—too many.

They stole deep inside, following the beat of my heart and the rush of my blood, beyond the heart link that bound Red and me, into the deep roots of my magic, velvet black as a cloudless night sky and filled with the stars that reflected the power of all the worlds—the power of creation itself.

They skipped beneath the darkness and wholeness of my magic, tumbling into my patched-together soul. Into the nest of spotted moths clinging to one another, antennae tasting and testing the air, wings fluttering and settling over and over again, mimicking the shape of my heart.

Pestilence had made a disastrous mistake.

Soul sickness could not infect me. The Angel held the alchemy of my soul safe. Even as the sparks caught on the wings of the moths, the Angel's cold smothered the fire.

I was immune. I belonged to *la Muerte*. Pestilence could not defeat us. We were stronger. More powerful. The most powerful of the Horsemen.

Too late, I realized my own mistake.

I might be impervious to the soul sickness, but not to distraction. Not to misdirection.

Mine was not the only soul I carried.

The single moth of Luna's soul broke from the others, winding and circling, wings driving. She wound her way toward me—toward the sparks of soul sickness—holy and fragile.

Vulnerable.

Not immune. Not immortal.

Gabriel's words came back to me in a rush.

If she dies a third time, all will be lost.

CHAPTER 13

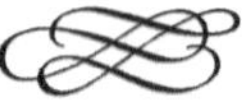

I F A SPARK OF SOUL sickness caught Luna's soul in this place—in the darkness of my depths, cradled within the magic of my heart, among the gathered souls of my victims—she would be bare and raw, with no flesh and blood to shield it from the pain the sickness would wreak. Nothing to break the wildfire that would ensue. Her worst fears would come to pass in the blink of an eye.

Her soul would burn, just as it had before. Only this time, there would be no coming back from it.

No going back in time, for we could go back no further. No archangel to save the day. No blood magic to slow the destruction.

Only a death that the Angel and I could not stop or reverse.

He couldn't help—no, he *wouldn't* help. The Angel's ice could not shield both of us. He had to choose. He chose me. It was that simple. That terrifying.

I reached for Luna with my magic, slipping through the edges of her soul. Flooding through her being. Measuring her memories. Looking for something—anything—with which to defend. The small, winged creatures that formed the shape of my soul took flight to place themselves between Luna and the fiery threat.

They would not get there in time. Not enough of them to make a difference.

Luna called my name, shaking me to my marrow.

Night!

I'd give anything to help her. I'd give it all. I'd take the full brunt of the soul sickness if I could. I'd let the spark catch. I'd let it burn, if it meant I could keep her safe.

The Angel's voice sounded within me.

That is not our place.

It had always been my place—to sacrifice myself, first on the altar of the Order, then on the altar of love. I took the body blows, the mortal wounds. I came within a heartbeat of dying. I did that so that others wouldn't have to. I owed it to them. I owed it to the souls that had given me the second chance.

You know what we have to do, the Angel said. *Luna's soul must be returned. There is no other way.*

To force Luna's soul back into her body—into communion with Pestilence—how could I do that to her? How could her soul live through that and remain intact? How could I tear her from safety and sentence her to suffer like that?

How could I live, knowing that I'd done something like that—not in the thrall of the Order, but of my own free will after having vowed that I would never murder again? Wasn't this the same, or worse, than murder?

Wasn't this what Michael had warned me about?

It was my greatest fear. My own worst nightmare. And there was no way out.

Safety is an illusion. A lie, the Angel said.

Even here, where Luna ought to be able to hide. Where she should feel protected. Where she should *be* protected.

I wished like hell that it could be so. But wishing wouldn't change the fact that one of two things would happen in the space of the next heartbeat.

Luna would die. Or Luna would live, but the price of living might be more than she could bear.

She continued to call my name. To ask for the one thing I could no longer give her.

I looked at her, and she at me. She read the truth in my eyes.

No, she said.

I shook my head. *There's nothing else. I'm sorry.*

Time slowed. The sparks that flew toward her seemed to float, but flew toward her still. The time loop that we'd been caught in—that Pestilence had shredded—shifting, changing, opening.

Luna dove this way and that, looking for an escape, but there was nowhere to go. I used my magic to still her, to steady her. I opened myself to speak with her in a way I'd never done with anyone before. Not Faith. Not Red. Not anybody.

Soul to soul.

Luna, you have to do this. If you refuse, we will force you. Do you understand?

She cringed, but couldn't backpedal. She couldn't move at all under my power. Her soul screamed.

I held on. I listened and I heard. I took the anguish in her cry into myself. I let it bludgeon me bloody, but I refused to let go.

She wailed until she had nothing left. Until all of her fight drained away. Then she sobbed.

The sparks moved inexorably forward, ready to light her soul. Ready to burn.

There's no more time, I said. *It has to be now.*

She went limp. Offered no resistance.

There was no grace here. No peace. Only terror that had overtaken her utterly. Fear had won.

I wanted to love, she said. A dying declaration spoken so softly, I barely heard it.

What? I asked. *What did you want to love?*

My life, she said. *My world.*

Her memories flashed in my mind's eye. Her first encounter with Charlie. The kindness she'd shown him. The hope she'd held when she'd first made her way to Addie's house. She still carried those thoughts and feelings within her. But she'd have to choose them. She'd have to choose hope in the face of every denial. She'd have to take it on faith that something good waited for her, even if that seemed impossible.

Do you still want to love? I asked.

The smallest spark kindled in the depths of her soul.

Then fight for it, I said.

There was nothing else.

The Angel wove his magic with mine, his icy grave and my darkness. Together, we caught Luna's soul like a moth caught in a child's hands in the twilight of a summer's night. We carried it along the veins of my magic, following the rush of my blood and the beat of my heart, onward and outward until we came to awareness on top of Pestilence.

The Horseman remained pinned by my weight and strength in the flow of molten rock, struggling to keep its face out of the fire. It maintained its grip on my neck. Squeezing. Choking. Driving its soul sickness into me as if it hadn't yet realized that there was nothing inside of me any longer that could be killed.

Only seconds seemed to have passed.

The Angel and I held Luna's soul at the ready.

What happens after we place her soul into her body? I asked.

Then it's up to her, the Angel said. *She will have to find her way.*

We can't help her?

Could anyone have helped you with me? the Angel asked.

I could slip into her mind. I could—

What? the Angel asked. *Invade the last shreds of her sanctity?*

But she'll have to fight Pestilence on her own. Without the knowledge, training, and experience I'd had to help me with the Angel. She was a fucking civilian. She'd been dragged into all of this against her will.

There had to be something I could do. Something that would make a difference.

I felt a pull on the heart link.

Red.

I couldn't turn my head. Pestilence's grip limited my line of sight. I could only feel for Red to zero in on him. To know where he stood,

To know that the light that shone from his sacred heart was blinding.

I took the body blows. The mortal wounds. I sacrificed so that the people I loved didn't have to. I knew what had to happen. I felt it in my gut.

I grabbed hold of Pestilence's arms and rolled off of the Horseman, bringing it with me. Allowing it to force me into the lava. To pin me down. To tighten its hold on my neck.

The Angel couldn't counter—not yet. We still had one thing left to do. One necessary, terrible thing. And it would leave us as vulnerable as Luna.

I whispered a prayer to the powers.

The Angel and I shoved my palm into Pestilence's chest with speed and magic, shoving Luna's soul back into her body, sending her to battle against Pestilence with nothing except her wits and her exhausted will.

This time, her scream shattered me. In it, I heard the death of hope. I felt desperation. The heartache in it couldn't be contained. It couldn't be compassed.

I let it burn me as I felt the burn of the molten rock on my skin. It melted and vaporized and disintegrated. I let it sear me into oblivion in that moment, drawing what absolution I could. I held on to consciousness long enough to watch Red shove his hands through the Pestilence's back, the light of the sacred heart overtaking them both.

CHAPTER 14

THE ANGEL'S ICE shielded me from the fire, making me whole almost as quickly as I burned. My awareness flickered in, then out, and finally in again as instinct took over where my thinking mind couldn't quite manage yet. I scrambled from beneath Pestilence and Red, rising to my feet, ready to take on the Horseman. To hold him still. To give Luna a fighting chance.

But Red had a firm hold on Pestilence's—Luna's—body. And this wasn't my battle to fight. It was Luna's. All I could do was witness.

My magic rose, faltering a bit as my flesh continued to knit back together. I slipped into the landscape of Luna's mind, but found no active thoughts. No active memories. Her mind reflected the scape where we physically stood. The molten rock. The molding of the world in the moment of creation. The breathless time before time.

I felt for her soul. I sensed the threads of its terror like the strands of a spider's web. I followed them down into her heart, which, like mine, would now be the seat of her magic. I plunged beyond the beat of muscle and the rhythmic flow of blood into her core, violating every single boundary of privacy a person could have, following until I found her.

Until I found them.

Magic that I identified as Red's held the space in which Luna's soul squared off with Pestilence's twisted intelligence in what appeared to be a boxing ring. Just the mat and the ropes. No referee. I was the only audience.

It smelled like a gym. Like sweat and dirty socks and rubber and blood. It sounded like Luna's heartbeat. *Thump-thump. Thump-thump.*

I tasted Red's magic in the air, grass and earth and something new. A love bigger than anything he and I shared. A love that could hold the whole world—all the worlds—in its arms.

I couldn't wrap my mind around it. It was larger than me. Bigger than anything I'd ever felt.

Red's magic had turned the ring a glowing red. His power evened the odds. It gave Luna ground to stand on, a foundation of love. Of compassion. Of strength. Of ferocity.

Love was as fierce as it could be kind. Love was justice. Love gave Luna a chance.

It was her only chance.

She faced Pestilence head on, her soul no longer appearing in the guise of a moth. She looked like herself, near to how I'd first seen her. The strip of dark hair crowning her otherwise shaved head. Freckles sprinkled across her cheeks and nose, her light brown complexion blanched. Black leather earrings cut into the shape of feathers brushing the tops of her shoulders. Dark gray hoodie, holey, faded jeans, and gray wool socks, capped off with black boots.

Pestilence no longer looked like her mirror image. It looked like a shadow. A malevolent darkness, hovering at the ready.

It snarled. "Get out."

Luna drew herself to full height, staring into the space where the Horseman's eyes should be. "I have nowhere else to go."

"Die, then."

"You tried to kill me. Didn't work."

"I'll try again."

She took a step toward it. "Why?"

Pestilence stepped back. Its mouth worked. It couldn't seem to answer the question.

"Why do you hate me?" she asked.

"Because you live," it said.

Luna nodded. "And now, because of me, so do you."

Pestilence froze.

Luna advanced again. "You hear me? You're alive now. Do you know what that means?"

This time the Horseman stood his ground. No backpedaling. No surrender. "I was made to destroy life."

"Sucks to be you, doesn't it?" Luna asked. "Alive, but created to destroy the living. What the hell are you supposed to do with that?"

The Horseman stared at her.

"Do you know what it means?" she asked again.

Pestilence shook its head.

"Do you want to?"

The Horseman trembled.

It wanted exactly what Luna offered. It wanted it so badly, that desire had become a hunger that had never been satisfied, a thirst that had never been quenched. Pestilence had longed for something that it had missed every single moment of its immortal life.

It had grown to hate what it couldn't have. Its hate was dangerous. Poisonous. It had to be reckoned with.

I saw it. I felt it. I knew it.

So did Luna.

"Do you want it?" she asked.

Pestilence didn't answer.

"There's a price, if you do. It won't come cheap."

The Horseman said nothing, but it listened.

"I'm in charge in here. This is my body. My life. My magic. I have to learn how to live with it, and you will defer to me in all things or so help me God I'll find a way to exorcise you. I don't care if everyone says it's impossible. Because after what I've been through over the last twenty-four hours, fucking nothing is impossible. Do you understand?"

Pestilence nodded once.

"Number two," Luna said. "You will heal everyone you've made sick. Everyone. There will be no lasting damage. No trace. They will be whole. Do you understand?"

The Horseman nodded again.

Luna took another step toward it. "Third and last—for now. In addition to deferring to me, you will defer to Night if what she asks does not contradict my will. I don't know anything about living with someone like you, but she does. I need her help. I need backup. I trust her. You will also trust her."

Pestilence hesitated. After a moment, it said, "You can't force me to trust."

"Fake it until you make it," she said.

"What?" it asked.

"Pretend. It will get easier."

It shook its head. For a second, it seemed as if the Horseman refused. "Why are you offering this to me? I'm everything you should fear. Everything you should hate."

"And I have everything you've ever wanted," she said.

"But why?" the Horseman asked. "I must know."

Luna turned her gaze to look at me.

I blinked at her. I hadn't realized she'd felt my magic. That she'd felt me watching.

"Because everyone deserves a second chance." She returned her gaze to the Horseman. "Do you accept?"

Pestilence's shaking grew more pronounced.

I knew how it felt to leave behind the only life you'd ever known—the hate and resentment, the fear and desire—to risk everything for the one thing you wanted most. The one thing you could exist without, but could never truly live without.

There was nothing more frightening. But there came a point where refusing to take that risk was worse than death.

Pestilence had to choose.

It answered from the core of its being, one word that rang out with all the power of all of time, changing the course of its destiny, and Luna's along with it.

"Yes."

CHAPTER 15

I JOGGED ACROSS the floor of Justice Gym, past barbells, plates, racks and pull-up bars, the interlocked black mats on the floor absorbing the sound of my steps. I breathed in the perfume of rubber, sweat, and cleaner, my skin thrumming with the beat booming from the speakers. The wind howled outside, rain falling in sheets, pounding like nails on the windows in the garage doors in back. A low rumble rolled across the sky, the sound so unfamiliar it took me a heartbeat to place it. Thunder.

A rare thing in Portland, but one that served well to mask our magic this morning. The more chaotic weather energy we could manage, the better the camouflage.

I bounded past the office, taking the stairs two at a time to the entry, glancing at the empty cubbyholes and the man-eating sofa before coming to a stop in front of the glass door. I pressed my hands against its chilled, smooth surface, studying the street.

The darkness before dawn looked the same as it always had. Tires slicked on wet pavement and engines hummed. Normals on their way to work grabbed breakfast and coffee at Stumptown Diner across the way. The Orange Warrior rode past on his bike, catching sight of me at the door and flashing a peace sign. He'd moved on before I could raise one in return.

I felt Red's presence behind me a moment before he threaded his arms around my waist. I breathed in his grass and earth, leaning into him. It felt different than it had during the time I now thought of as Before. I couldn't quite get to the contour of his body the way I remembered it because there was more of me now. The wings that had only just begun to grow in after our fight with the End had filled in all the way. Even folded and tucked against my back, they took up some space that both of us would need to get used to.

That was the price I'd paid for doing what was needed. That, and the Angel's constant presence. I'd worried for Luna because I thought I'd known what she'd signed up for. I'd been full of shit.

Luna seemed as all right as she could possibly be, given events. She and her Horseman had spent the last three days and nights at Addie's, getting used to the feel of each other and healing the household of any lingering magical sickness. Then she'd wanted to make sure that she could move through the world without making people sick, too.

No one had wanted to come with us this morning. I couldn't blame them for not wanting to spend time with the being who'd cursed them if they didn't have to.

Red kissed the back of my neck. "I'm gonna want some time alone after this is done. Do you think we could take a day?"

"If the Apocalypse lets us," I said.

"The Apocalypse can go fuck itself."

His lips wandered to the side of my neck, to the spot behind my ear. It had the desired effect—I melted into him.

"Yes." I turned to face him.

The lines in his forehead seemed to have multiplied over the last week. His eyes looked tired, but held a spark nonetheless—a mix of love, lust, and concern.

I combed my hands through his shaggy hair and brushed his mouth with mine. "I'm here."

"I know," he said. "You promised you'd come back to me no matter what happened. I knew you would."

"Then what's the worry? Besides the obvious ones, of which there are many."

That earned me a small smile. "I have a question for you. The timing's not good—when could the timing ever be good right now?"

"What kind of question wouldn't you come right out and ask?"

He took his time answering. "One that's traditional when you love somebody and want to spend the rest of your life with them, no matter how long—or short—that life turns out to be."

My mouth fell open.

A flash of light behind Red, followed by the stink of sulfur, curtailed anything I would've said.

He frowned. After a moment, he planted a kiss on my forehead and spun on his heel, leading the way down the steps to the gym floor, where a portal had opened, dislodging a handful of people. Some of them, I felt more glad to see than others.

Faith's gold-and-silver halo flickered with a god's power. In every other way, she looked like my kid, from the shine of joy in her brown eyes to her cornflower-blue sweater, black jeans, and black boots. She'd pulled her long waves into a ponytail. My hourglass pendant dangled at her throat. She wrapped her arms around me before I could do the same, squeezing me tight, stealing the air from my lungs before she finally let me go.

"Staying or going?" I asked.

"Staying," she said. "For a couple of days."

Just what I'd hoped to hear—or close enough.

Corey waited behind her, her fire-engine-red bob catching the overhead light. She wore black-and-white stripes from shirt to skirt to tights to match her black-and-white skull cameo rings and earrings. She looked happy, at least for now. If she ever made it home, her parents would probably ground her for the rest of her natural life.

Kevin the Faery King had come as well. The portal was his magic, created painstakingly to connect this space to a safe place within his realm—one with enough invisibility and protection to house a Horseman of the Apocalypse and his human vessel, away from the prying eyes and prying magic of pissed-off archangels.

He seemed both in and out of his element, an eighteen-year-old kid who'd seen too much and given up his humanity to make sure the rest of us could hold onto ours. He'd swapped his leather vest and pants for a denim jacket and jeans, his white T-shirt matching new white sneakers. If it hadn't been for the white wings, he might've been any kid in the world. In one hand, he carried two enormous black backpacks by their top handles.

"One of these is mine, Night. Other one's for you."

I raised a brow.

He turned to Corey. "Would you?"

She helped him put the pack on. And slip his wings inside the damn thing.

"Seriously?" I asked.

He inclined his head toward my back. "You're going grocery shopping with those free and clear for all to see?"

I nodded once, giving him the point. "Thanks."

"No worries," he said. "Where's our passenger?"

Red answered. "Be here in a minute, along with Charlie."

I smiled at Kevin. If we got the time, it would be good for us to talk more. I got the feeling he thought the same.

The last of our visitors stood with his hands in the pockets of his black leather trench coat. He wore a black tank beneath it, black leather pants, and black motorcycle boots on his feet. A black wool cap covered his bald head. He met my gaze with gray eyes, his mouth pressed into a hard line. He had no halo, but the feel of power around him was undeniable.

I'd promised him that I'd do everything in my power to stop Pestilence from taking a human vessel, and I'd done exactly that. He feared what could happen if all of the Horsemen became embodied in this world. Understandable. But it was just that—a fear, not a certainty.

I refused to let my own fear stop me from doing the right thing, let alone his.

"Hi, Malek," I said.

He raised his hands to sign. *I don't like how this turned out.*

I shrugged. It was what it was.

I don't blame you, he said. *But Michael will.*

"Probably," I said. "But I'm not here for Michael. He wanted control. We gave him something better."

He won't see it that way. He wanted to strike a blow against the End.

"This wasn't about Michael or the End," I said. "It was about Luna. I'm not playing the pawn in some celestial power game. None of us should."

Malek grinned. *You're in trouble, Night. You* are *trouble.*

"Guilty," I said.

It's my kind of trouble.

I wasn't sure how I felt about that. I wasn't here for Malek, either. I had my own path to walk. I had my own reasons.

Another sulfur bomb exploded in the air a half-second before the space beside me parted with a *pop.* Charlie and Pestilence—Luna— stepped through.

Charlie had gotten his clothes washed. He looked downright spiffy, ready to take on the task of gathering the magical children from his time and bringing them forward into ours, where they would be healed of their soul sickness. Where they could be as safe as we could make them. Where they would be needed.

Luna wore clothes borrowed from Addie. She looked solid in dark blue jeans and a navy blue tunic, her dark Mohawk gelled to its full glory. Her mirrored halo shone with pale green flecks.

"Excellent," Kevin said. "We need to move right now. The longer y'all are in the same place—Night and Luna, that is—the easier it will be for Michael or Gabriel to sense you, regardless of how badass your protections are. Everyone ready?"

"Not quite," Charlie said.

Kevin shook his head. "Make it quick."

The kid hugged me. When he pulled away, his eyes looked suspiciously wet. "See you soon, Night."

"Take care of yourself." I ruffled his combed hair and enjoyed the side-eye he shot me.

He stepped aside to make way for Luna, who met my gaze with a grace I'd never have believed possible. I prayed that if anyone could find a way to be all right in this, it would be Luna.

I started to say the words that had come to mind every single day since we'd been back. I opened my mouth, but nothing came out.

"Don't," she said. "I've been watching you try to work up the nerve to tell me you're sorry. I don't care whether you are or not. Just don't say it, okay?"

I understood. It didn't matter how I felt about what I'd done. It only mattered how Luna felt. She got to choose, and I respected her decision.

"Okay," I said. "If you need us—the Angel and me—all you have to do is call. We've got your back."

"I know." She glanced over her shoulder at the group that had come for her. "They look shifty. You sure I can trust them?"

It took me a second to realize she'd made a joke.

"Most of them." I leaned forward to kiss her cheek, and lingered to whisper. "I mean it. If you need anything at all."

She turned her head, pressing her brow to mine, gazing at me through her lashes. "I'll call. I promise."

I would hold her to it.

Kevin cleared his throat. "Now?"

I took Luna by the shoulders and turned her around.

Red took my hand, and together we watched as Luna stepped through the portal, followed by Charlie and Malek, with Kevin bringing up the rear. Thunder pealed and lightning flashed as the opening melded into a seamless, hidden door to which only the four of us still present knew the key.

I took a deep breath into the sudden silence. We had quiet, and we had peace. It wouldn't last long, but I'd take what I could get.

I turned to Red. "About that question?"

Faith looked at me, then at him. "What question?"

I had eyes for Red, and Red alone. I studied the lines on his face, the fall of his hair, the curve of his cheek, the bow of his mouth. He stood only inches away. I felt the heat of him on my skin. I wanted him for now and always.

Before we heard an unexpected knock on the door, before Michael or Gabriel or anyone else could intrude, before the next maelstrom stirred—I needed him to know.

I leaned into him, meeting his evergreen gaze, and whispered my answer against his lips.

"Yes."

He kissed me hard, lifting me off the ground.

My heart took flight.

If you enjoyed this book, please consider leaving a review. It doesn't have to be long—even a few words will be very appreciated.

Reviews make it possible for an author to continue writing books in a series. They make a big difference in helping to get the word out about a book or a series. And reviews can make the all difference in the world when a reader wants to take a chance on a new author, but isn't sure whether they will like the book.

Thank you for taking hours out of your busy life to read. I hope this book brought you time to escape into a story, and that it brought you joy.

Turn the page to read Chapter 1 of **Angel Roars**, Book 5 of the *Soul Forge* series.

ANGEL ROARS - CHAPTER 1

RARE SUNLIGHT STREAMED from the clear blue sky, a benediction for my sleepy neighborhood. The ice coating the bare branches of the maples along the street glittered like diamonds. I inhaled January frost, my exhale fogging the air. The tips of my fingers felt chilled inside my black leather gloves. I hadn't gotten used to the pack on my back or what it camouflaged. The melting slick on the sidewalk made temporary peace with the soles of my boots.

Peace. What a strange word. An uncommon feeling.

Beside me, Faith slipped, catching her feet a split second before she tumbled into the snow piled at the curb. Her cheeks flushed with the cold as she held out her arms to help with balance. Her long black hair gleamed in the morning light, her brown eyes filled with humor. Bundled up in her black down coat and wool scarf, matching wool mittens on her hands, she reminded me of her younger self. She'd been a child once. Not anymore.

The halo that enveloped her body—an expression of her life force and magic—shone equal parts silver and gold. The silver had been hers since she'd been born. The gold belonged to the god she carried inside, the Awakened.

It had only been a month or so since the Awakened had come alive within her. Since she'd gone from being only my daughter to becoming the vessel for the god of magic itself. She'd spent most of that time in Texas, creating a safe space for other magical children. Having her here in Portland, even for a couple of days, meant everything.

We'd left Red at home in his pajamas, building a fire in the hearth, promising to bring back breakfast and coffee from the winter wonderland. The kiss he'd given me before I'd stepped out the door and locked down its magical protections glowed with so much warmth and promise, I hadn't wanted to leave home.

Home—another strange word.

He had his own place, and I had mine, but we'd spent most of our time of late at a friend's house, fortified against the forces of evil, fighting to stave off the oncoming Apocalypse. No one had time for snowy mornings and leisurely breakfasts and family. We'd all been too busy making hard choices. Surviving.

"You're thinking about it again," Faith said. "You should stop."

"The rest of the worlds aren't going away. We have enemies. We have to stay alert."

She sighed. "It's your training. If you were a normal, you'd be talking about the glorious sunshine."

"If I were a normal," I said, "a lot of things would be different."

I hadn't been a regular, non-magical girl, though. Not since I was a toddler. My ability to meld my consciousness with other minds had come on hard and fast, disturbing my parents' sense of good and evil and taking us all down a dark, narrow road to Hell.

In the end, they'd been killed. The Order of the Blood Moon—an order of magical assassins—had become my family. They'd taught me strategy and obedience. They'd taught me to use my magic to kill, and all the blood on my hands had shattered my soul.

I'd left them behind years ago, going on the run with Faith. By the grace of the powers and the spirits of the dead, my soul had been created anew. Still, my Order training hadn't left me. If anything, I relied on it more every day.

We rounded the corner, moving from the quiet of the neighborhood onto Hawthorne. The street wasn't as busy as it should be because of the snow and ice. There were more pedestrians than cars. Lots of families out and about. The parents looked relaxed, released from their workaday routines. The kids looked overjoyed.

A block or so ahead, in the shadow of newly built apartments, the coffee shop's sign shone brightly.

"We've been left alone for less than a week," I said. "No Order assassins. No magical attacks. No archangels on the doorstep. That won't last long. It's hard to let it go."

"Thirty minutes," she said. "Can you do half an hour?"

I looked at her. "Why?"

She slowed to a stop. "Because I miss you, Night. I have a job to do, and I'm going to have to go back to it. The time will fly and this will all be over. I want to spend some time with my mom. You know, like most people. Regular people."

I adjusted the straps of my pack. Most people carried stuff in their backpacks. Most people didn't have a full set of black-feathered angel wings folded down to a compact twelve inches, hidden underneath waxed canvas and Italian leather. Most people didn't serve as the human host of the Angel of Death.

La Muerte—the Angel—laughed. The sound echoed inside my head and rumbled inside my chest.

Once upon a time, he'd been my prisoner, then my passenger. Now, I didn't know exactly what to call him. We were becoming one, he and I. I feared how that would turn out for me. For the people I loved.

I had a lot to worry about. Faith was asking me not to spend my thoughts and energy on any of it for thirty lousy minutes. I could do that. Couldn't I?

I took a deep breath and blew it out in a stream of fog and mist. "Okay."

We walked into the coffee shop, which had its heat cranked up to a level that reminded me frogs could be convinced to boil to death. The tables to our right had been taken by computer people, the sofas and comfy chairs to our left peppered with readers and conversationalists. Nate, the brown-eyed kid with the lady-killer smile behind the counter in front took orders, an army of three behind him to execute.

The sounds system played a series of Linkin Park tunes. The line was short, and the people unremarkable. Everyone in their proper place, eyes on their own business or staring off into space, daydreaming. The short hall that led to the restrooms and back exit was clear.

We'd arrived just in time—a group pushed through the door behind us, filling up the line, pulling off hats and gloves, murmuring amongst themselves.

A normal coffee shop. A place for regular people with their shiny non-magical halos.

After a couple of false starts, Faith asked for three bacon-and-egg sandwiches and three coconut-milk lattes. She wandered off to the side to wait while I fished crumpled cash from my front pocket.

Nate pitched his tenor low, for my ears only. "You see that guy in the corner?"

I raised a brow, taking my eyes off my palm full of money to meet his gaze. "What?"

"Something's wrong with him."

I glanced over my shoulder, zeroing in on a bearded guy in a green knit cap and matching coat. He leaned against the back wall, go-cup of coffee in hand, lost in his thoughts. His white skin looked pale, the lenses of his silver wire–framed glasses casting shadows beneath his eyes. The corners of his mouth turned down, trembling. He shifted his weight from one hiking-booted foot to another. His halo had no shine —no, he had no halo.

No, that wasn't right.

His halo had been overtaken. Overwhelmed by nothing at all.

Nate's voice interrupted my thoughts. "I don't know why I'm telling you this, except that you look like you can handle yourself. Like you'd know what to do with that guy."

I looked at him. He pressed his lips together and kept his jaw square, as if he were trying to keep it together, but his eyes held a wildness that reflected the truth—that he was freaked out.

I handed him a twenty. He made change as if there was nothing wrong.

"Keep it," I said.

He shoved three dollar bills into the tip jar. "What do I do?"

"Give the breakfast order to Faith when it comes up. I'll check out your trouble."

His relief was so immediate and thick, I could've cut it with a knife. "Thank you."

"Don't thank me yet," I said.

I tried to catch Faith's eye, but she'd glanced down at her phone, thumbs racing across the surface. Judging by the softness of her expression, she was texting her girlfriend, Corey. She wouldn't look up without my touch or my raised voice, and I didn't want to draw attention.

I started toward the trouble, my magic rising with me to fill every cell, every molecule, until it pushed up against the edges of my skin. I held it in check, ready to strike, ready to slip into his mind and bind him to the spot where he stood if necessary.

He blinked, climbing out of his imagination and into the present. He raised his chin, meeting my gaze with unexpected boldness for a stranger.

There was nothing in his eyes. Not a single emotion. Not a coherent thought. He looked empty, but he smiled at me. The gesture made my skin crawl.

I sensed no magic in him. No power that he could unleash in this place. But every inch of his nothing-halo screamed that he was a threat. That he, and he alone, could hurt me. Hurt Faith. Harm all of us.

I picked up my pace, making a beeline for him. Placing myself between him and as many people as I could shelter with my body and my power.

He turned on his heel, dropping his go-cup, which exploded in an espresso-and-foamed-milk bomb on the floor. The people closest to him leapt out of the way in a cascade of *whoas* and laughter and scrape of chair legs on concrete. He shoved his way through the people in line and out the door.

I threaded my way through the crowd to follow, stepping out into a gust of icy wind, my feet unsteady on the slick sidewalk. I looked left, then right, catching sight of my target standing in front of the bright blue taqueria next door.

I sent my magic barreling for him, sliding into his consciousness and pinning him to the spot where he stood.

The sight of his own reflection in the taqueria window captured him. He marked the hat and coat, the fact that his glasses felt crooked, and the way his skin looked bleached, as if all the blood had drained from his face and hands.

His name was Mark.

His last memory was of stepping out his front door this morning, keys to his truck jingling in hand, and heading up the salted slope of the sidewalk to the apartment parking lot. A crow cawed from its perch in the ice-laden, bony branches of the oak behind the building. The wind kicked up, blowing from the Columbia River Gorge in the east, whipping the branches into a clacking, crackling frenzy. The wind seemed to find every seam and space in his coat, chilling him to the marrow.

His girlfriend had been out of town for a week, and he was headed to the airport to pick her up. He couldn't wait to taste her sweet mouth and run his hands through her long brown hair. A week was too long.

Then he'd spied the woman from 7B, a nurse heading home from her overnight shift. She liked to wear pink scrubs. They looked good on her.

He'd moved aside on the walk to give her the right of way—it was only polite, and he'd been raised to care about that. She'd laid a hand on his arm as he smiled in greeting, which was weird. Usually she kept her hands in her pockets.

His vision grayed out. For a second, he thought he might pass out. Maybe he was having a heart attack. Maybe a seizure.

Didn't make sense.

Then his vision blacked out. There was nothing else. Nothing until he'd somehow come to, standing in front of the taqueria window, staring at his reflection.

He knew where he was. He ate at this place a couple of times a month. He loved the pollo verde. He loved the chips and salsa. He especially loved the horchata. But he'd been on his way to the airport, not on his way to breakfast tacos. He plucked his phone from the back pocket of his jeans. No, he only thought about it. His arms and hands refused to obey, as if he'd frozen to the spot. As if someone else had taken control of him.

That was a crazy thought. This was the real world, and that shit didn't happen here.

Fear bloomed in his heart like a poisonous flower as I came to stand in front of him, blocking his view of the window.

His halo had shifted in the time it'd taken me to walk to him. Where before there had been nothing, now the normal shine reasserted itself—health and vitality returning. A sense of self. A sense of consciousness.

I met his gaze, searching him for any signs of magic. There were none.

He wanted to ask me who I was. What I'd done to him and why.

I let go of him, noting the fine motor movements as his own systems of balance and being took over again. He blinked at me.

"Are you Night?" he asked.

My turn to show surprise. "Have we met?"

"No," he said. "At least I don't think so. But I know your name. And I know that you're Death."

He said it just like that—with a capital D.

"What happened to me?" he asked.

"I don't know," I said, although it wasn't one-hundred-percent true.

He acted as if he'd been possessed, but I couldn't tell him that.

He swallowed hard. "Can I go now?"

I had no reason to hold him—at least, none that I could see right now. He was already freaked out. Judging from the tremor in his fingers, not too far from being on his way to panic—or rage.

I opened my mouth to invite him to sit down. I'd buy him a new cup of coffee and we could sort things out with more time and space, although I had no faith that more of either would give us better answers.

The words died on my tongue.

As I glanced past him, I caught sight of a familiar figure across the street, bundled in a black leather jacket and leaning against the side of an empty, darkened bar. He bore all of his weight on one black-booted foot, the other braced against the wall. He'd hooked his thumbs in the front pockets of his black jeans. The once-white script emblazoned on his black T-shirt read, *Ride the Lightning*. He had black hair, short and thick.

For a heartbeat, his hair appeared to be made of fire, writhing flames of orange, yellow, red, and blue. He had three eyes, two in the usual places and a third in the center of his forehead. He wore glittering, diamond-like armor, a sword with a golden hilt sheathed on his back.

Then his normal-guy façade returned. He could've been anyone—except for the way the air bent around his body in response to the immense power he carried.

"Go on," I said absently to Mark.

He didn't need to be told twice. He walked away as fast as his feet would take him, leaving me standing on one side of Hawthorne and the archangel Michael on the other.

AUTHOR'S NOTE

I love all forms of story, from books to movies to plays. I love folktales told by the light of a campfire and spectacular Hollywood blockbusters in which there are so many explosions that "Explosions" should be listed as a character in the credits. I feel the same way about paintings and drawings and sculpture. And music. So much music.

All of that is to say that, as much or more as I'm a creator of art, I'm a capital-F Fan. There are few things I love more than losing myself in someone else's art, and the number one force that drives my love of art is connection.

You might have noticed that very short dedication at the front of this book: *For Chester*.

High on the list of bands whose music I love is Linkin Park, and Chester Bennington was the band's lead singer. He died in July, and it broke my heart. I never met him, and I never got a chance to see the band perform live, but none of that matters in the end. The connection forged through the music is what matters. Helping each other is what matters.

I wrote *Night Strikes* while listening to Linkin Park's music. In fact,

I listened to nothing else for months. Although I listened across their entire catalog, I can say unequivocally that their album, *A Thousand Suns*, was and is a huge blessing for me, and that I was listening to "Iridescent" with tears streaming down my face as I typed the last words of the book in a small upstairs room at an inn on the Oregon coast.

2017 has been a very difficult year. There have been hardships, untimely deaths, natural disasters, and catastrophes created by human beings as well. There has been enormous change. The special headspace I enter when I write—which, for me, is almost entirely the rocky underground of my subconscious mind—has sometimes felt hard to access. But I do the work of excavating there anyway, because that is where my deepest hope lives. And damned if we don't need all the hope we can get.

Every artist I know has expressed something similar.

Alongside my greatest hope lives my greatest fear, of course. Usually, I find a way to dance with it so that I can return from the deep with the treasures that become words on the page.

That's how it works for me. That's how it's always worked. With *Night Strikes*, however, something different happened.

I typed, "The End." I sent the finished draft to my wonderful first readers, who are also terrific writers and friends, and spent a week handling other things, including herding cats at my day job (that's my official title there: Cat Herder). I handled all of the other stuff that goes by the wayside when I'm writing. And then I got a phone call about the book.

My friend and first reader said, "You realize you forgot to write the climax of this novel, right?"

I hadn't realized that at all—not until she told me. I mean, the climax of a book is its reason for being. Why would I leave out something so important?

For a good reason: I would have to delve into particularly tender places in my subconscious in order to write the climax of *Night Strikes*, and I just plain didn't want to do it. I didn't want to dance with the fear this time.

But I couldn't leave the book without a reason for being.

So, I had a good laugh on the phone with my friend. And then I canceled my pumpkin-carving plans for that afternoon, put on some Linkin Park, and breathed through the dance. In the process, I healed a part of my broken heart.

I learn something new with every story and every novel, which is really a polite way of putting it. It skims over the hard work, making it look effortless even if it was anything but. A dear, departed friend of mine had a better take, and I'd rather put it his way.

Writing this novel, like every other meaningful life experience, was AFOG—another fucking opportunity for growth.

As they say, everyone you meet is facing a challenge you may know nothing about. So, please, be kind to yourselves and each other. And when we fall down, let's help pick each other up.

Wishing you stories, magic, and heart,
    Leslie
    November 26, 2017

ABOUT THE AUTHOR

Since the age of seven, Leslie Claire Walker has wanted to be Princess Leia—wise and brave and never afraid of a fight, no matter the odds.

Leslie hails from the concrete and steel canyons and lush bayous of southeast Texas—a long way from Alderaan. Now, she lives in the rain-drenched Pacific Northwest with a cast of spectacular characters, including cats, harps, fantastic pieces of art that may or may not be doorways to other realms, and too many fantasy novels to count.

She is the author of **The Faery Chronicles** and **Soul Forge** series, two complete series of urban fantasy novels, novellas, and stories filled with found family, angels, assassins, faeries, and demons.

Connect with Leslie
leslieclairewalker.com
leslie@leslieclairewalker.com

ALSO BY LESLIE CLAIRE WALKER

THE AWAKENED MAGIC SAGA

THE SOUL FORGE

(The Complete Series)

Angel Hunts

Angel Rises

Angel Falls

Angel Strikes

Angel Roars

Angel Burns

THE FAERY CHRONICLES

(The Complete Series)

Faery Novice

Faery Prophet

Faery Sovereign

SHORT STORY COLLECTIONS

(Set in this World)

Faery Tales Volume I

Faery Tales Volume II

COPYRIGHT